A PRIDE CHRISTMAS

JILL SANDERS

To my family

SUMMARY

Take a magical trip back to Pride, Oregon. Meet some new people and watch how the Jordan family welcomes them in this special holiday novella.

Alice McKinney was supposed to be home for the holidays, enjoying her mother's homemade pies and her father's fried turkey. Instead, she's trapped in a blizzard, holed up in a small cabin somewhere on the coast of Oregon. If that wasn't bad enough, her brother had sent his best friend, Eric, to drive her home instead of coming himself, which means she's stranded with the man of her childhood dreams.

It was supposed to be a simple road trip to help his best friend out. Go down to Cali, grab Alice, and bring her home to Portland. Spending fourteen hours in a car with the girl he'd always wanted but couldn't have was punishment enough. Then the storm hit, leaving them stranded in a romantically perfect setting. Now, he'll get to spend the holidays with his dream woman in a very magical place.

CHAPTER 1

Alice stared down at the black Mustang and frowned.

"Well?" Eric said impatiently. "Are you going to get in or just stand there and get soaked?"

Her brother, Chris, had sent Eric Jenkins to pick her up from school and drive her the fourteen hours home, which pissed her off. Especially when Eric continued to sit in the warm dry car instead of jumping out and helping her haul her luggage down the pathway and put it into the trunk.

"Trunk's open," he called out to her through the crack he'd opened in the window.

She ground her back teeth and growled as she quickly made her way through the California rain, trying to avoid some of the larger puddles in the pathway as she hurried. Putting her three bags in the trunk, she narrowed her eyes at the back of his head.

Two of her friends had had to help her carry her suitcases down the dorm stairs, and when she bent over and tried to lift the largest one into the trunk, her back cried out in protest. She grunted loudly and tossed the thing in, slamming the trunk as hard as she could.

She could just imagine Eric hissing at the abuse of his "baby."

Jumping in the passenger side, she made sure to shake the raindrops from her hair, letting them splatter the interior of the car. He hissed and wiped the dashboard dry with a small yellow cloth.

"Why are you here?" she asked through her clenched teeth.

He stopped wiping the dash and looked over at her. "To get you," he answered slowly, as if she was dense. "You did want to go home for the break, didn't you?"

"Yes, but Chris was supposed to drive me there. Not you."

He shoved the yellow cloth back in the glove box and started the engine. "Well, Chris had a change of plans, so you got me instead." He shrugged as he pulled out of the parking lot.

"What other plans? He is going home, right?" she asked, worried that she wouldn't be able to see her brother during her break.

She'd been away at college a few months and needed this family time. She'd expected school to be hard but hadn't planned on being so homesick. Even though she and her brother went to school in the same state, three hours and lots of traffic between them meant she didn't see him much. As a matter of fact, she'd only seen Chris a handful of times since she'd moved to California and even less the couple of years before that after he'd gone to school.

The fact that she hadn't seen Eric for almost that long as well hadn't escaped her. Eric Jenkins had been her very first crush. To this day, her heart skipped every time she was in close proximity to him.

He was everything she'd ever dreamed about: her prince, her leather-wearing biker, her football superstar, and her beach-bum god in nothing but swim shorts. He fit the bill for every fantasy she'd ever had.

Back in middle school, Chris had scolded her and told her she was being too weird around his friend and to knock it off.

Over the years, as her infatuation with Eric grew, this… annoyance had grown between them. She'd started thinking of it as sexual tension and fed off of the attention.

Now, however, she was truly annoyed that Chris wasn't there to get her. After all, she was wearing a cozy pair of yoga pants, her worn Ugg boots, and an oversized UCLA sweatshirt. Her dark hair was tied up in a loose bun, which was tucked under a heavy beanie.

If she'd known Eric was coming, she would have made sure to look much better.

She held in a gasp when she realized she wasn't even wearing makeup. Was it too late to run back inside? She glanced out the window and realized he'd already turned onto the highway. Damn. She was going to have to keep her face turned away from him for most of the trip. Maybe if they stopped for gas, she could run in and apply the basics.

"This is a first," Eric said easily as he got into the fast lane on the 405 heading north.

"What?" she asked, trying to keep most of her face turned away from him.

"You… quiet." He chuckled.

Her eyes narrowed as she turned to him. "Don't you have something better to do than drive me all the way home?"

"Nope," he said easily. "So, what is it? A man?" he asked, continuing without a hitch.

"What?" she asked, her heart skipping as she looked at him.

He was dressed in worn jeans and a black sweatshirt. It was hard to tell if his dark hair was long or short at the moment since he was wearing a ball cap. He looked like the epitome of her college boy fantasies.

"Are you quiet because of a man? Did you break up with him?" he asked, then gave a faux gasp. "Did he break up with you? Inquiring minds want to know." He smiled at her.

"Shut up," she said, crossing her arms over her chest and glaring out the window.

"So, it was a boy." He paused. "Or am I totally off here? Was it a girl?"

"No," she answered easily.

"No to the boy or the girl?" he asked, and she could hear the curiosity in his voice.

"Neither," she said, wishing he would just shut up. She was finding it hard not to be charmed and knew that the fourteen-hour drive would be absolute hell if she fell even harder for him.

"Alice, it's going to be a very long trip if we don't talk," he finally said a few minutes later. "You can't be that mad at Chris."

"Why can't I?" she asked, her arms still over her chest.

"Because it was sort of my idea," he admitted, shocking her.

"Why?" she asked him, feeling the tables turn.

"Because…" He darted a glance in her direction. "He wanted to spend time with Dawn and…"

Whatever else he had to say, she blocked out.

"Chris ditched me so he could spend the time with his girlfriend?" She almost squealed it out, causing Eric to hiss.

"I… didn't… no…" He shook his head. "You can't tell your folks that he ditched you. Not yet."

"Why not?" She jerked her head towards him, totally forgetting about her bare face.

"Because I promised…" He sighed. "Please? Don't say anything to them?"

She could see the plea in his eyes. No matter what she thought of Eric, he'd always remain a good friend to her brother. She only wished she had friends of that caliber.

"Fine," she finally groaned. "But just because I'm pissed at him and he's not here. Of course, you know this means you'll be getting the second degree once we get home."

"Nope, I'm going to drop you off and then head home myself." He smiled.

"I thought your folks moved to Arizona."

"They did, but my sister and both brothers are still in Portland. I'm spending the holidays with them and my nephews. All three of them." He smiled.

"How is everyone?" she asked. She'd seen pictures on social media of his older sister's new baby, Joshua. His brothers both had sons too. There wasn't a girl in the bunch.

"It's the first time I get to meet the little guy. I'm told he reminds her a lot of me." His smile grew bigger.

"Then your sister and Mike are in big trouble," she said sweetly. She glanced out the window again as the car sped along the interstate heading further north.

CHAPTER 2

Eric laughed at Alice's joke. God, why was it so easy and hard at the same time to be around her?

She was the only woman he'd ever felt comfortable talking to, but also the only one who made his palms sweat and his heart race.

He'd been avoiding her since she hit fifth grade, when he'd noticed just how long her legs were and how she'd filled out her swimsuit at Chris's birthday party at the water park. She was two years younger than him and he'd been infatuated with her ever since that summer. When Chris had caught him flirting with her, he'd promised his friend that it was just harmless and that there was nothing behind it. He'd steered clear of her ever since, even though his infatuation had grown over the years.

He'd known she had a thing for him back in high school. It had been easy to tell since she'd blushed every time she was around him. But one day he'd caught her making out with Roger Linsey, and their relationship had changed to what it was now.

"What?" she said after a long silence.

"Hm?" He glanced over at her. She looked even better than the last time he'd seen her. Her hair was longer and a shade of caramel brown that made her brown eyes look larger somehow. Even though it was all piled on her head in a loose bun, he still had an urge to reach over and touch it. The yoga pants she was wearing forced his mind to wander to all the other places he'd like to touch as well.

"What? You're obviously upset," she said, crossing her arms over her chest. Which made him think about her breasts. His eyes jerked back to the road when an impatient driver honked at him for not going ten over the speed limit.

"No," he replied. "Not upset."

He heard her sigh and could just tell that she had rolled her eyes.

"What was that for?" he asked.

"I call tell you're lying. Seriously, we've known each other since we were five."

"You were five," he corrected. "I was seven."

"Whatever." She sighed again. "We've known each other long enough to know when the other one is hiding something."

"I'm not upset," he reaffirmed. "Just… deep in thought."

"About?" When he didn't answer, she groaned. "It's a very long trip. Very long and I bore easily."

He chuckled. "I was thinking about Roger Linsey."

"Who?"

His eyebrows shot up. "High school… Junior Prom?"

She surprised him by laughing. "I'd forgotten about that." She scooted further down in the seat. "Fun times."

"What ever happened between you two?" he asked.

"Why do you ask?" She looked at him and waited.

"I…" He had nothing. "Just curious."

She rolled her eyes. This time he saw it. "We dated for about a week, that was all. What happened to Julie Hawthorn?"

He didn't remember who Alice was talking about but figured it was one of the many girls he'd dated in school.

"Same," he said easily.

They were silent for a while. "How's school treating you?"

"Good," she said too quickly. "You?"

He shrugged, realizing he shouldn't have started the conversation if he didn't want to talk about it himself.

"Hanging in there," he admitted.

"That doesn't sound good."

"Only a year left." He groaned.

"What will you do then?" she asked.

"Not sure." He glanced over at her. "You?"

"I still have a few years left to decide." She actually sounded eager and excited, and he realized that there were more differences between them than just age.

"You're taking classes for…" he asked.

"Physical sciences," she answered enthusiastically. "Chemistry, geology…"

He remembered she'd always been great at the sciences. "So, any particular field you're interested in?"

"There are so many options. Too many, that's the problem." She tucked her feet up on his dash and rested her arms on her knees as she glanced out the window.

The snow continued to fall and had slowed down the

traffic to the point that it was going to add an extra hour to their trip.

"At least you have options," he hinted.

"True." She smiled. "You'll have plenty of options as well with your degree in engineering."

"Yeah." He swallowed the knot in his throat. "Sure."

"What?" she asked. He glanced over at her. "You had a tone."

"No tone," he replied.

"Oh please." She chuckled.

"Can you believe Chris wants to sign up for more school?" He tried to change the subject.

"He wants to go for his bachelor's in health," Alice answered.

"Yeah, crazy." He shook his head thinking about his best friend, how they differed. Chris had always been great at school, just like Alice.

"He's always loved school."

"The two of you were always too smart for the rest of us," he admitted.

She chuckled. "If I remember correctly, you and Chris were always neck and neck in school."

"Not always," he admitted begrudgingly.

"How about lunch?" she asked when the traffic came to a stop. "If we get off the highway now and grab some food, maybe this will clear up by the time we're done."

"Great idea." He started moving across the highway towards the exit. "I'm sure there's a place around here."

They found a little diner near the highway and had soup and sandwiches while the traffic continued to crawl by the windows.

When they got back in the car, the traffic was moving more swiftly, and the conversation turned to their families.

His sister and two brothers were all married and living their own lives. His older brother Nathan had his first child on the way. Sarah and Mike had their son Joshua, while Joe, who was only a year and a half older than Eric, had two kids, Aiden and Evan.

Being the youngest of the group had always meant that he lagged behind everyone else.

Just before nightfall, they hit Sacramento and he pulled over once more to fill his car while she rushed into the gas station to use the restroom and grab some snacks.

After filling up, he walked in and grabbed some chips and a bottled water.

"Won't you need more than that to stay awake?" she asked, nodding to the water.

"Nope," he answered. "I was hoping you would take the wheel for a while."

"Sure." She motioned to the large soda in her hands. "I slept for a few hours, so I should be good to go."

CHAPTER 3

Alice couldn't help but sneak peeks at Eric while he slept. Sure enough, he was even sexier asleep than when he was awake. She kept her mind busy as she drove towards home, thinking of her parents and being home for her first holiday since she'd moved out. She'd spent Thanksgiving with a few of her new friends. A large group of them had gone to a little lounge in downtown Santa Monica and then had wandered over to the beach and ended up at Pacific Park.

It hadn't really felt like Thanksgiving, since it had been in the seventies and they had eaten at a little fish lounge that specialized in tourist food. Even with all the festive decorations and music pumping through the speakers, she'd missed Oregon and her family. Which was why she'd asked her brother to drive her home this year for the two weeks' vacation she needed.

Where was Chris anyway? Was he on his way home? She'd texted him, but, so far, he hadn't responded.

She glanced over at Eric again. He would know. When

he woke up, she'd have to pump him for information about her brother.

The last time she'd seen Chris, he'd been dating someone named Dawn and had hinted that it was getting serious. Was he still dating her? Oh god! Was he bringing her home for Christmas so the folks could meet her? If so, why wouldn't he have wanted her along for the trip? Something wasn't sitting right with her and the sooner Eric woke up, the sooner she could get answers.

Seeing that the gas had reached a quarter of a tank, she decided to pull off at the next exit and hit the gas station.

When she finally pulled in under the bright lights of a gas station, she'd been driving a little more than four hours.

Before she could jump out, however, a gas attendant knocked on her window, waking Eric up.

"Where are we?" he asked instantly.

"Just outside of Roseburg." She rolled down the window and told the attendant. "Fill it up." He nodded and disappeared.

"Right." Eric stretched and rolled his shoulders.

"I'm heading in for a bathroom break and a coffee. Want anything?" she asked.

"I'll head in as well." He followed her inside and shopped around while she disappeared into the bathroom.

When she came out, he was at the register paying for the gas and some food.

She grabbed the largest coffee cup and filled it up, then took a breakfast burrito from the heater, making sure to check the date.

"I just made those," the woman behind the counter called out to her in a friendly tone.

"Wonderful." She smiled and took another one, wondering if Eric had grabbed one for himself. She took her coffee and the burritos to the front and paid.

"You two heading home for the holidays?" the woman asked.

"Yes." She smiled.

"Are you heading north or south?"

"North," she answered as she signed the credit card machine.

"I hope you don't have too far left to go," the woman said, handing back her credit card and receipt.

"Why?" She frowned as she tucked them back into her purse.

"You're going to run into problems early morning. There's heavy snow just outside of Eugene. You'd be better off heading over on the one-thirty-eight and hitting the coast the rest of the way up. Eugene's supposed to get at least a foot of the white stuff before daybreak. After that… even more. It's going to be a very white Christmas for a lot of us around here."

"Thanks." She took the bag with her burritos and her coffee.

"I told your man there the same, but he seemed half asleep still." She nodded to the large window.

"Yeah," she agreed. "I'll pass it along to him," she said as she stepped out.

Sure enough, she could feel the change in the wind as she walked towards the car. Already the rain had turned, and very light snowflakes were drifting slowly down, melting almost instantly on the warm ground.

Getting back in behind the wheel, she set her coffee

down in the cup holder and pulled out a burrito while the attendant finished cleaning their windshield.

"What's that?" Eric asked, frowning down at the food.

"Breakfast burrito," she answered, with her mouth full.

"That looks and smells amazing." He started to reach for the handle, but she held up the bag.

"I got one for you." She handed over the bag.

"Really?" he asked, suddenly more awake.

She wiggled the bag. "Going once…" He snagged the bag quickly from her fingers, making her chuckle. "Men." She shook her head and rolled down the window to hand the attendant a few dollars. "Thanks." She smiled at him before rolling her window back up and pulling out of the station.

She finished her burrito just as she pulled back onto the highway. Within fifteen minutes, Eric was asleep again, having finished off his burrito and a whole bag of potato chips.

By the time she hit the Route 138 turnoff, the snow was falling faster than the wipers could clear it off the windshield. Glancing over at Eric, she made a quick decision and took the turnoff. It would add several hours to their trip to drive along the coast and then head back inland to Portland, but she figured they would easily make the time up avoiding the storm.

If the weather had held, they'd be less than three hours from home. Part of her didn't want the car trip to be over that soon. She was pretty sure that once Eric dropped her off at her parents' house, he'd disappear to his sister's house or one of his brothers' places, and she wouldn't see him again for another year.

Almost a full hour later, what was left of her coffee

was too cold to enjoy. She pulled into another gas station in Reedsport. This time, Eric didn't even stir when she turned off the engine.

When she opened her door, the brisk freezing air hit him and he sat up.

"What?" He glanced out the window at the whiteout. "What the hell?"

"It's snowing," she answered. "And that coffee ran right through me. I'll be back." She ducked out and disappeared into the gas station.

She took her time reapplying some makeup and brushing through her hair, then she stepped out and glanced towards the car. Wondering if Eric had gone back to sleep, she paid for the gas and stepped outside.

When she saw him sitting behind the wheel, she cringed, wondering if he'd be mad at her for the detour.

"Where are we?" he asked, but the tone in his voice told her that he knew exactly where they were.

She swallowed. "Reedsport," she answered cheerfully and put on her seatbelt.

"Why are we in Reedsport instead of Portland?" he asked, his knuckles turning white on the steering wheel.

"There was snow and… the woman at the gas station told me that Eugene was supposed to get bombarded with it. So I took her advice and went this way to avoid the storm." The words rushed out of her as she opened her soda and took a sip.

"The most up-to-date weather report just said that it's going to miss Eugene and hit the coast instead."

She cringed. "Oh, well, we can always hit the one-twenty-six back over to I-five." She glanced out the window as the snow continued to fall in fat flakes.

"If it stays open." He turned on the car and pulled out of the station.

Twenty minutes later, the snow was getting so bad, Eric had taken to cursing under his breath every few minutes. Sure enough, Route 126 was closed due to whiteout conditions.

More than three hours later, they had traveled less than a hundred miles with no way back to the main highway, which had been reported to have closed less than an hour after she'd taken the turnoff.

"Either way we would have been stuck," she said softly. "At least this way, we're a lot closer to home than if we'd stayed on the highway." She held on as the car started sliding.

"Easy," Eric said to the car. "Just a little more." He'd been promising his car that for the past hour.

"Why don't we pull over? Find a place to wait the storm out?" she suggested. "There's a little town…" She pointed to the sign, showing that it had all the amenities. "We can spend the night here and still make it home in time. It's a full week before Christmas. How long can a storm last?"

"Yeah," he said after the car slipped on ice again. "We'd better pull over, I guess." He turned the wheel and almost put them in the ditch. "Son of a…" He gripped the wheel tighter.

"Are you mad?" she asked, once they turned into the small town.

"No," he said softly. "Like you said… we made it farther than if we'd stayed on the highway." He pulled into a small grocery store's parking lot. "I didn't see a hotel. Did you?"

"No, maybe someone inside knows of a place," she suggested. "I'll go in…" She reached for the handle.

"No, I'll go." He jumped out before she could tell him she had to use the bathroom again.

She followed him into O'Neil's Grocery and smiled when the woman behind the counter welcomed her.

"It's a rough day to be out in this," she called to them both.

"Yeah," Eric sighed. "Know of any place we can wait the storm out?"

"Well, now, are you two honeymooning it?" the woman asked.

"No," Eric denied quickly. "Just trying to head home for Christmas."

"Oh, well, Pride Bed and Breakfast is the only place with availability." The woman smiled. "I've got a flyer right here." She held it out. Alice moved quickly and took it from the woman.

"Bathroom?" she asked quietly.

"Just down the hallway." She motioned towards the back. "You might want to stock up before you head out. Megan has some supplies, but it never hurts to have extra before the roads close."

"Good idea," Eric said. "I'll grab us some supplies." He motioned towards the hallway. "Go."

She didn't wait but disappeared down the hallway.

Spending more than a dozen hours sitting in a car drinking was making her look like she had a very small bladder.

CHAPTER 4

Eric filled a shopping cart with everything he thought they would need for the night, including frozen dinners and a bottle of wine for later.

He was paying for all the food when Alice walked back out from the hallway. She looked even fresher than when they had walked in. He was pretty sure that half of the time she was in the bathroom she was applying more makeup and fixing her hair. Now it lay in a long braid over her shoulder. She'd changed from the oversized sweatshirt to an off-the-shoulder sweater during one of their stops.

She was still wearing the tight yoga pants and her Uggs, but with the changes she'd made, she looked even more amazing than when he'd picked her up from her dorm yesterday.

"Ready?" he asked her.

"Yes," she said, eyeing the four large bags he had in the cart.

"If you two need anything else, let Megan know. Oh,

and tell her Patty sent you." She winked at them. "Drive safe."

"Thanks again," Alice said over her shoulder as she followed Eric outside.

She bumped into his back when he stopped after the doors closed.

"We'll have to carry these." He motioned to the bags. "I doubt the cart will make it through this."

There was easily another inch on the ground than when they had walked in. He reached in and handed her the lighter bags and then took the heavier ones and carried them across the parking lot.

When Alice slipped in the snow, he almost dropped a bag when he helped steady her by taking her elbow.

"Easy," he said, holding onto her while juggling both bags in one arm. "It is really slick out here."

"How is it that so much snow can fall so fast?" she said when he set the four bags in the trunk alongside their luggage.

Instead of getting back in the car, Alice stood by the passenger door, looking around the small town.

"What a cute town," she said, getting his attention.

He glanced up and, for the first time in hours, took in the sights. She was right. There were Christmas lights and decorations on every street post going down the main street. The buildings lining the main road were old but very well maintained.

He could make out the town square, where a huge pine tree was covered with colorful lights. The entire square was decorated, in fact.

"Yeah," he agreed, feeling the chill sneak in through

his heavy jacket. "We'd better go. If there isn't a spare room…"

"There is. I called while you were paying." She smiled. "It's not a room, though. We have our very own cabin." She opened the car door and got in.

He started the car and followed the directions she gave him, heading back the way they had come. The roads were even worse than before and when they finally reached the turnoff to the small road, he was feeling relieved that she'd talked him into turning off.

They passed a couple of larger homes and then came to a massive white two-story place with green shutters. He parked. There was a large sign that read Pride Bed and Breakfast.

"Nice place," Alice said, leaning forward to look at the house. "I guess the cabins are that way." She motioned to a pathway, which had been cleared of most of the snow.

"Yeah," he agreed and thought about carrying all of their bags and groceries down the walkway.

"Here comes someone," she said, getting his attention. Sure enough, there was a man bundled up in a black wool coat, hat, and gloves heading towards the car.

By the time he stepped out, the man was beside the car.

"You must be the Jenkins," the man said easily, holding out his hand. "I'm Todd Jordan. My wife and I own the B and B." From what he could tell, the man was about ten years older than he was.

"Eric." He shook the man's hand.

"Ma'am." Todd turned to Alice, who had also climbed out of the car. "I can help you cart your things down to the cabin if you need a hand."

"Sure." Eric walked around and opened the trunk.

The man chuckled. “Just like my wife. She can’t go anywhere without at least three bags,” he said as he took the two larger of Alice’s bags.

He thought about telling the man that they weren’t married, but something told him to hold back. After all, what did it matter? They were probably only going to be there for a night.

“Thanks,” he said after he grabbed his own bag and Alice’s smaller one, then tucked a bag of groceries in his free hand.

“I’ll get the rest.” Alice stepped forward.

“Are you sure. I can make another trip?” Todd asked.

“Yes, I’m fine.” She shifted the bags until she could get all three of them in her arms.

“Got everything?” Todd asked.

“Yes, thank you.” Alice smiled up at him. “You have a lovely place here.” She motioned to the house.

“You haven’t seen the best part yet.” He nodded to the pathway. “You’ve got the cabin with the best view. Even during a snowstorm, it’s pretty incredible,” he said as they started walking down the path. “You lucked out. We had the place booked, but the couple that was supposed to be here for this week got snowed in and couldn’t make it. The rest of the cabins are booked, so if you get lonely…” He shifted her two bags as they continued down the path. “If you want to go for an outing, we serve dinner from five-thirty until seven-thirty up at the main house. But it looks like you guys stopped in town and stocked up at Patty’s place.”

“Yes,” he answered. “We didn’t know what would be available.”

“Smart thinking. I’ve had people stuck in storms like

this without so much as a ketchup packet in their car." He shook his head as they passed the first cabin. The bright green paint on the door seemed an almost shocking color next to the blinding white of the snow around the quaint little building.

He was sure hoping that their cabin was bigger than that one. They passed two more cabins that they could see from the pathway, each one bigger than the last one.

"Here we are." Todd slowed down and nodded to a larger cabin with a bright red door. There was a big porch on the front of the place. The lights were on inside, making it appear warm and welcoming.

"I started a fire in there for you after you called. It should be nice and toasty by now," Todd said, stepping onto the front porch. "There's that view." He nodded behind him.

Alice gasped, causing him to turn around. Sure enough, the Pacific Ocean sat just a hundred yards from them. Large waves crashed against the shore and rocks while the snow continued to fall in huge fluffy clumps.

"It's even better on a sunny day," Todd said, opening the door and stomping his feet on the doormat.

"Well, this place is yours for as long as you need it." Todd set the bags down just inside the door.

When Eric stepped in behind Alice, the warmth of the fireplace hit him, removing all of the cold from outside.

"It's wonderful," Alice said cheerfully. "Thank you."

"Sure thing. There are some basics in the fridge and cabinets, but it looks like you two have the rest covered." He took two of the bags from Alice and set them on the counter in the small kitchen. "If you need anything, just let me know. I'm going to try to keep the path cleared, but from the looks of it, the white stuff is coming down faster than I can shovel." He chuckled.

"We're good. Thanks," Eric answered in reply.

Todd moved towards the door. "The number to the main house is there." He pointed to the phone. "Enjoy yourselves."

"Thanks," he and Alice said at the same time.

When the front door shut behind Todd, the room was silent for a moment, then Alice began moving around the kitchen, putting the cold items in the fridge.

As the silence stretched on, he walked around the cabin and was thankful to find that there were two small bedrooms. Seeing the one bathroom in between had him cringing, but he knew it was better than any hotel they would have gotten.

He walked back over to the front windows and stared out as the snow continued to fall.

"I'll take the room on the right," Alice said behind him, picking up one of her bags. He moved quickly to grab the bigger one, but she already had her hand on the handle, and he ended up covering it with his own. Touching her was like touching an electric fence; he could almost see sparks shooting from their joined skin. He felt it vibrate up his arm and shoot into his chest.

"Sorry," he said softly and jerked his hand back. "I'll carry these in for you."

"I can do it myself," she said, her chin going up slightly. "After all, I did carry them to your car myself."

"Right." He remembered sitting in the car while she waddled through the rain yesterday. "Sorry," he said again and watched her drag her bags towards the back rooms.

He watched the snowfall for a moment, thinking about

being stuck with Alice for a full night. There had been plenty of times when was younger that he'd spent the night over at Chris's place. But back then, Alice had been his best friend's annoying little sister. When he'd started thinking of her as something else, they'd been too old for sleepovers.

He'd been avoiding her for a good reason. He'd never felt the way he felt about her about anyone else.

Even on a simple car trip like they were on, he'd laughed more than he had with any other woman. She was easy to joke with, to talk to, to be around. It just felt right. Her.

Not to mention the spark that always happened when he was around her. It was like being too close to the speakers at a concert. She made his entire body vibrate.

Glancing at his watch, he pulled out his cell phone and shot a text to his sister, telling her that he was delayed.

When he heard the lone shower turn on, he instantly wished for a shower himself. But knowing Alice and remembering how Chris always complained about how long his sister took in the bathroom, he figured he had some time. He decided to take a walk and stepped out onto the porch and took a deep breath. Coughing instantly from the chill coming off the Pacific, he bundled his jacket around him and set off towards the beach.

CHAPTER 5

The hot shower felt wonderful. She thought of Eric as she stood under the spray for almost ten minutes. Then, shaking the thought of spending the night under the same roof with him, she used the fancy guest shampoo and conditioner and cleaned up. She'd taken plenty of road trips in her life, and the best part of each one had been when the travel was over. But this trip hadn't been that bad, mainly because of the conversations she'd had with Eric.

It had been years since she'd spent the night under the same roof with Eric. Chris stopped having him over shortly after his thirteenth birthday.

Alice had always believed it had something to do with her flirting with Eric, but her brother had never mentioned anything about it.

What should she do now, she wondered, wiping the mirror free of fog. Her long wet hair hung around her shoulders. She didn't want to spend the time to blow dry it, since she was just planning on eating something and crawling into bed to catch up on some sleep.

She pulled on a fresh pair of yoga pants, a tank top, and a sweater. She took a few extra minutes to braid her hair and apply the lightest makeup so she didn't appear too homey.

But when she stepped out into the living room, he wasn't there. Nor was he in the other bedroom. Walking over to the windows, she noticed his footprints in the snow, leading down towards the beach.

She walked into the small kitchen to see what she could drum up for food. By the time Eric walked back into the cabin, she had a full pot of spaghetti and was pulling garlic toast out of the small toaster oven.

"Wow," Eric said, removing his jacket and hat, then sitting down on the side of the sofa and pulling off his shoes. "What's all this?"

"Dinner," she answered, feeling slightly embarrassed.

"You can cook now?" he asked, setting his shoes on the mat by the front door. They were covered in snow and sand. His dark hair was still dry, since he'd been wearing a beanie, but the tip of his nose and ears were a little red from the cold.

"I made some coffee too." She nodded towards the hot pot. "I figured you'd be cold when you came back."

She had set the small dinner table and had even found some candles to light.

"The fire needs more wood." He tossed a few logs on it before stepping up to the table. "It's a good thing I thought to grab this." He held up a bottle of wine. "She turned and smiled at him "You pour?"

"Sure." He chuckled.

She finished putting the bread on the table and scooped some spaghetti onto their plates. She made sure to add an extra scoop onto his, since she remembered how much he ate.

When he handed her a glass of wine, she was sitting at the table. "Thanks," she said, feeling nervous.

"This looks amazing. Chris never mentioned that you'd finally learned to make something other than mac and cheese," he joked.

"Chris has been away at college for the past few years," she supplied then sipped the wine. "How was your walk?" she asked, hoping the alcohol settled her nerves.

"Cold." He laughed. "But amazing." He took a bite and groaned with pleasure.

"Good?" she asked, feeling even more nervous. She really hoped he would like it.

"Very," he agreed and took another bite. "I was so tired of potato chips and soda." He reached for his wine glass and took a drink. "Now, if there was some beer in that fridge" She shook her head. "I didn't think so." He took another sip of his wine. "Still, you can't beat a home-cooked meal."

"Does it look like it's letting up out there?" She looked towards the dark windows.

"No." He frowned. "I checked the weather apps and it actually shows we could get two feet tonight."

"Two?" She almost dropped her fork.

"Yeah, they're expecting even more tomorrow during the day. We may be stuck here for a few nights."

She shrugged. "Thankfully, we have a full week before Christmas." She smiled. "Chris is stuck in LA. All flights to Portland were canceled."

"He was going to fly?" Eric asked, sounding a little surprised. When she'd talked to her mother and found out that her brother was flying up instead of driving, she'd assumed Eric had been in on it.

"Yes." She frowned. "Didn't you know?" He shook his head and continued to eat.

"Did you talk to him?" he asked between bites.

"No, I called my mother and told her we were stuck."

Eric cringed.

"What was that for?"

"Nothing." He shrugged. Her eyes narrowed and he sighed when she gave him her "I'm not buying it" look. "It's just… your folks… they know you're with me?"

"Yes," she said slowly. "Why?"

"I don't think your father likes me," he said quickly.

"Of course, he likes you. He's known you your entire life. My parents are practically your second parents." She waved him off.

"No, your mom loves me," he corrected. "Your father on the other hand…" He suddenly shut his mouth and shook his head.

"What?" She set her wine glass down without taking a sip.

"Nothing." He took another bite and picked up a slice of bread. "This is really—"

"Eric," she interrupted him. "What? Why do you think my father doesn't like you?"

He sighed and looked at her. "Because he sees how I look at you."

She felt as if she'd been hit in the gut with a sledgehammer.

"How?" she asked softly.

"You know how." His eyes locked with hers.

"No, I don't." She shook her head. "Tell me."

Instead of answering, he just sat across from her, watching her. The heat from his eyes as they ran slowly over her had her body vibrating with want. She'd always wanted him. Would always want him.

"Eric?" His name was a whisper on her lips.

The chair scraped as he stood up quickly. Her eyes followed him across the room. He stood for a moment, looking out the window.

"I promised myself I wouldn't do this," he said, keeping his back to her. "I swore to Chris—"

"My brother isn't here," she said quickly, causing him to turn around.

"Obviously." He groaned and turned away again. "If he was, he'd punch me in the gut just seeing the way I look at you."

"I look at you the same way," she said, standing up. Their food on the table was all but forgotten as she walked across the room and stopped next to him. The beauty of the snow falling in the spotlight of the porch went unnoticed.

She touched his arm. "Eric." Before she'd finished his name, he had turned and wrapped his arms around her. He pulled her close until, finally, his lips covered hers in the most perfect kiss she'd ever experienced.

He released her just as quickly as he'd taken her in his arms, his taste still on her lips. She wanted more. A lot more.

But when she reached for him, he jerked away. "Go to bed," he said, turning away from her again.

"No." She stopped herself from stomping her foot.

"I'm tired of playing games. My brother has nothing to do…" He glanced over his shoulder at her.

"You don't want to finish that sentence." He almost growled it out. "Chris is my best friend, first and foremost."

She swallowed the hurt that had welled up in her chest. "He's not—"

"I won't betray his trust," he broke in again. "Go." He waved towards the back of the cabin. "I'll clean up."

Turning quickly, she almost walked out of the room empty-handed, but then she backtracked, grabbed her glass of wine, and marched towards her bedroom. Stopping once more, she turned and, as he watched her, she took the entire bottle of wine with her as she disappeared into her bedroom. She thought she heard him chuckle behind her, but she was too angry to care.

Slamming the door behind her, she leaned on the closed door and finished the first glass of wine. Then, still feeling pissed, she had another one for good measure.

CHAPTER 6

He needed a cold shower, but since he was still chilled from the long walk, which had been meant to clear his mind and body from wanting Alice, he settled on a warm one instead.

Tucking the towel around his hips, he cursed under his breath when he realized he hadn't brought any clothes with him into the bathroom.

Piling his dirty clothes in his arms, he opened the bathroom door and almost dropped them when he saw Alice standing just outside, the empty bottle of wine in her hands.

Her eyes ran from his face down his body slowly, causing whatever water drops were left on him to evaporate.

"Go…" he started to say, but she stopped him by telling him to go to hell. "What was that?" He was slightly shocked. He'd never heard her curse before.

"You heard me." She glared at him. "Go to hell." She

wobbled slightly on her feet, telling him that she really had drunk the entire bottle of wine.

"Alice," he said softly, hoping to try another tactic.

"Eric?" she asked, shaking her head slightly, then leaning against the wall for support.

He chuckled. "Yes?" He crossed his arms over his chest and decided to wait her out. It was only a matter of time before she either sank to the ground, a drunken mess, or threw up. Either way, he would be ready for it.

"You..." She waved the bottle at him, almost hitting him in the head. Luckily, he ducked and it grazed his shoulder instead. "You," she started again, "aren't allowed to kiss me like that."

"Okay," he said slowly, sobering. "I shouldn't have kissed you," he agreed.

"No." She waved the bottle again. This time he easily caught her wrists in his hands and took the bottle from her. He set it in the bathroom, far away from her, so he didn't get maimed.

"No." She shook her head. "You don't get to kiss me... *like that*." The last words were almost a whisper, as if they were a secret.

"Okay." He shook his head. "Like I said... I'm sorry..."

"NO!" She waved her arms and raised her voice. "You don't get to kiss me like..." She sighed and closed her eyes. "Like Wesley kissed Princess Buttercup."

He shook his head and smiled a little, knowing how to get a rise out of her. "Who?"

Her eyes narrowed as if she'd been challenged. "*Princess Bride*." She waved her hands again and he realized just how animated she was when she was drunk. "You know…" She cleared her throat and he remembered that she'd taken theater in school. Leaning back, he waited for the performance he guessed was coming. "Since the invention…" she started. It took her two tries to say *invention* and he smiled. "…of the kiss," she continued, "there have been five kisses that were rated the most passionate, the most pure…" His smile fell away. There had been nothing pure about the kiss he'd given her. There was nothing pure now or ever about his thoughts towards her. "This one left them all behind," she said after her eyes locked with his.

Shit, he thought. Hell.

"Go back to bed," he said softly. When she shook her head, he broke in. "You don't want to be around…"

He was shocked when she stepped forward and plastered herself against his wet chest. The thin white tank top she was wearing got soaked by the water droplets that hadn't evaporated from the heat of his body yet. Her arms wrapped around his shoulders.

"Kiss me like that again. Just once more…" She leaned up on her toes and gently touched her lips to his.

Had she done anything else, he would have had the willpower to deny her, but feeling those soft lips tenderly touch his, he was lost.

Dropping all of his defenses for a brief moment, he forgot everything.

"Alice," he said when she reached for his towel. His hands gripped hers to keep them from pulling the towel free. Resting his forehead on hers, he shook his head. "I…"

"Chris will never know," she said, her brown eyes begging him.

"I'd know. There's no way anyone would see us

together and not know. Besides…" He took a deep breath. "I have this fear that if I touch you once, I'll never stop."

She smiled quickly, showing him the cute dimple next to her mouth, the one he'd dreamed of kissing for years.

"Then don't." She tried to move his towel again, but he easily held her still.

"I have another policy; I don't take advantage of drunk women."

"I'm not that drunk," she added, rolling her eyes.

"Oh yeah?" He smiled. "Say the word invention again."

She narrowed her eyes at him in response. He chuckled. "You didn't finish your dinner." He'd cleared the dishes and put the leftovers in the fridge. "Why don't you go in, heat it up and—"

"I don't want food," she said, taking a step back. "I want you. I've wanted you for as long as I can remember."

He'd felt the same way but knew that there was no way he'd be able to live with himself if he allowed things to continue. He had promised Chris.

Taking a giant step away from her, he bent to pick up the clothes he'd dropped to the floor. She moved closer to him. Tossing the clothes on the bed, he turned back to her. "Let's go get you something to eat. Even if it's not the spaghetti."

"I don't—"

"I bought a carton of ice cream." He smiled when her eyebrows shot up.

"Mint chocolate chip?" she asked.

"Of course." He smiled and nudged her towards the kitchen. "I'll put on some clothes…" She turned back to him, hunger in her eyes. "Alone. I'll meet you in the other room." He pushed her playfully towards the kitchen.

He pulled on a pair of his sweats and a T-shirt and walked into the other room. She was sitting in front of the dying fire with the entire carton of ice cream, and two spoons, in her lap.

He tossed a couple more logs onto the embers and sat next to her.

"Here." She handed him one of the spoons, pulled her feet up onto the sofa, and opened the lid.

"I'd forgotten you took theater," he said, taking a scoop of the ice cream.

"Junior high and high school." She sighed as she took a bite. "I wanted to take acting classes at college, but…"

"What?" he asked after she shrugged.

She turned to him slightly. "I showed up and watched them practicing for a play they were putting on. Everyone was so much better than I was." She took another scoop.

"If my memory serves me right, you played the lead in almost every play."

"That doesn't mean I'm that good. We only had two hundred kids in our high school. There were easily a hundred people in the theater class." She frowned.

"It's not too late. Besides, just because you're not the best doesn't mean you couldn't have learned something new. That is what college is all about." He nudged her shoulder.

"Besides, my schedule was seriously hectic."

"Now you're making excuses." He set his spoon down and leaned back on the sofa, suddenly really tired. The stress from driving in the deep slick snow had worn him out.

"Not really," she answered. "I guess I just… grew out of it all." She shrugged and he could tell she was really thinking about something deeply. "Even school." She shook her head as if she hadn't meant to say it out loud.

"I thought you were really excited about school?" He asked, thinking of how she'd talked about it earlier.

"I'm just… tired of it all." She glanced at him sideways.

He leaned up again. "Of school?"

"Yeah." She set the carton down and wrapped her arms around herself. "I thought college would be like high school, only… better."

"It's not?" he asked, knowing his own experiences. He'd never been as good at school as Alice and Chris, but he managed to keep straight A's with a lot of arduous work.

"No." Her eyes moved to his. "I suppose I miss my old friends."

When she moved closer to him, he stood up and took the ice cream back to the freezer. "Alice." He turned and realized she'd followed him. He almost bumped into her. He took her shoulders in his hands. "I can't do this."

"Can't or won't?" she asked softly.

"Both," he answered. "Besides, I'm very tired." He figured that would stop her. Her eyes moved to the dark windows and he watched her shoulders slump.

"I suppose we're going to be stuck here for a few days."

He watched the heavy snowflakes falling in the light outside and agreed. "Looks that way."

Without a word, she turned away from him and started walking to her room.

"Night," he called out.

She stopped in the doorway. "This isn't over," she said softly before shutting the bedroom door.

No, he didn't think it was. Not when they were going to be stuck together in one of the most romantic settings he'd seen in a long time.

Throwing a few more logs on the fire, he decided to settle on the sofa for a while and watch the flames. His body was tired, but his mind was going a million miles a minute.

He pulled out his phone. Since Chris was grounded in LA, he'd probably be asleep already, but he shot off a quick text to him anyway.

-Snowed in somewhere in Oregon. Found a B&B to crash at. I don't know how long we'll be stuck. Heard you got grounded in LA.

He was slightly surprised when his phone rang instead of a text coming back to him.

"Hey," he answered Chris's call.

"Hey, I heard it's pretty bad up there."

"Yeah." He glanced towards the windows. "It's still coming down. We already have about a foot and a half."

"Mom was really upset when I told her we probably won't make it there until just before Christmas."

"Us?" he asked curiously.

"Yeah. I was bringing Dawn home. It was supposed to be a surprise, but since we're snowed out…"

"You're serious about this one?" he asked, glancing towards the back room, hoping he wasn't too loud.

"Yes." Chris's tone turned toward excitement. "I think she's the one."

"So, why not drive her up with Alice? That way the two of them—" Chris's chuckle stopped him.

"Alice and Dawn on a car trip? No thanks. Besides, Dawn could only get a few days off from work. We were set to fly out, but now our flights have been put on permanent hold. At least until the storm slows down."

He sighed and wondered if he should tell his best friend about his thoughts towards Alice.

"What's wrong?" Chris asked.

"Nothing," he answered automatically.

"Dude, I know you too well. I can hear that brain of yours cranking. Did something happen with Alice?" His friend's tone turned eager.

"No," he lied.

"She's okay?"

"Yeah, she's asleep. She made spaghetti and finished off half of a carton of ice cream."

"That sounds like her." Chris chuckled. "Then what is it?"

He frowned, remembering the kiss. Not the first one, but the second one. The one she'd given him.

"See, there it is again. That long silence. You're never quiet unless you're deep in thought. Just spill it."

"She kissed me," he blurted out without too much thought.

Chris shocked him by laughing. "Bout time."

"What?" He sat up and then for good measure looked at his phone screen to make sure he was really talking to Chris. "Who are you?"

Chris's chuckle continued. "Dude, that promise I made you give me was so many years ago. Alice is no longer my teenage sister who has a crush on you. She's her own woman and if she kissed you, she probably had a good reason. Besides, even my dad knows how you feel about her, and he's normally one of the densest guys I know."

Eric chuckled at that. Chris had always joked that he and Alice had gained their good grades and intellect from their mother.

"He once got his foot stuck in a bucket," Chris added with a chuckle, causing Eric to laugh along.

"Do you remember the time your dad decided to do some home maintenance and accidentally cut the electric wire, shocking himself?"

"I swear my dad took lessons from that tool man show."

"*Home Improvement*," he added with a laugh. "Yeah, every time he'd pull out his tools, your mother would groan and try to call a professional."

"Still does," Chris added, then he sighed. "Seriously though, if Alice kissed you…"

"Yeah," he sighed when Chris didn't continue.

"So?" Chris asked after a moment.

"So…" He leaned back and watched the fire. "This doesn't change us. You're still my best friend."

"Always," Chris added. "You know too much, and I have a lot of dirt on you, so we're stuck with one another."

Eric smiled. "Right back at you."

"Be safe. Stay where you are until the weather turns. I don't want to think about you two trying to get up to Portland in this stuff. From the weather channel reports, it looks nasty and appears that it's only going to get worse."

"We're not going anywhere," he agreed. "You and Dawn take the same advice."

"Yup, if we can't make it up to Portland, we'll try for her family in Georgia."

Feeling finally like he could sleep, he said his good-bye. He made sure the fire was mostly out, closing the glass doors on the fireplace before turning in for the night.

CHAPTER 7

When Alice woke, she instantly regretted not making sure the curtains were shut on the windows when she went to bed. The snow was still falling in thick clumps and with the brightness of everything outside, the bedroom was lit up like an operating room.

She pulled the covers over her head, wishing she hadn't drunk the rest of the bottle of wine, too. Her bladder was full, and she was pretty sure that the wood floor of the cabin was going to be cold. When she couldn't avoid the trip to the bathroom any longer, she debated taking the thick warm comforter with her on the trip.

Deciding against it, she climbed out of the bed and rushed across the floor. The hallway was a lot warmer than her bedroom and so was the bathroom. When she stepped out of the bathroom again, she glanced into the living area and saw Eric bent over the fireplace.

"Morning," he said over his shoulder. He smiled as he took in her appearance. She hadn't even looked at herself in the mirror. Still, she was too tired and cold to care at the moment. Moving closer to the fire, she backed her body up to its warmth.

"It's still falling out there." She nodded to the large windows.

"Yes." He took a throw blanket from the back of the sofa and wrapped it around her shoulders. "I made coffee, but there's also hot chocolate."

"Marshmallows?" she asked, stifling a yawn.

"I found some," he nodded.

"They think of everything, don't they?" She motioned to the cabin.

"Yeah," he agreed and moved over to make her hot chocolate. "So, what do you want to do today?" he asked as he waited for the single-cup maker to finish.

She glanced out the window again. "It might be nice to go for a walk sometime today."

"There are some games to tide us over." He motioned to a bookshelf full of old board games. "Or movies…"

She thought about spending an entire day with Eric and the only thing that kept running through her head was how sexy he'd looked last night in the towel. Thankfully, he had his back to her so he couldn't see the look she was giving him. Then she noticed his butt in the jeans he was wearing and bit her bottom lip.

Maybe she should just jump him? Would he let her get away with it? After all, he was the one who had kissed her first last night.

She hadn't realized he'd moved until a cup of hot chocolate with several large marshmallows appeared in front of her face.

"Have you decided yet?" he asked her as she took the mug from him.

"I think"—her stomach growled—"I'll decide after breakfast. But, if possible, I would like to get a walk in sometime today."

"Sure." He sat across from her. She was still standing with her butt towards the fire, enjoying the heat that soaked through the blanket and her yoga pants.

They sat in silence for a while, enjoying the hot drinks before he surprised her by saying.

"I talked to Chris last night."

Her eyebrows shot up. "And?"

"And, he and Dawn were going to fly up to Portland for Christmas."

"He *was* bringing her." She relaxed. "I knew it."

"Yeah, but their flight has been put on hold until the weather changes. They may end up going to visit her family in Georgia instead."

Her shoulders sank. She'd really wanted to see her brother this trip. Even if he was bringing a woman home with him.

"Does that mean it's even more serious than we all thought?" she asked, somewhat to herself.

"Sounds like it," Eric commented. "He's never brought someone home before." It was nice and strange at the same time that he knew so much about her family. After all, he had spent most of his childhood shadowing Chris.

"No, he hasn't. It really must be serious." She set her empty mug down. The room had warmed up by then. Setting the blanket back on the sofa, she thought about making something for breakfast. He'd purchased eggs and bacon at the store the night before. But first she wanted to change and get ready for the day.

"Go," Eric said standing beside her. "I'll cook breakfast, you get dressed."

"Thanks," she said before disappearing into the bedroom again.

When she came out, the entire place smelled of bacon, and her stomach responded with a loud growl.

"I may not be able to cook a lot of different foods, but breakfast is easy enough," he said, setting a plate down in front of her.

He'd made a smiley face out of the bacon and eggs, making her laugh. He set a glass of orange juice down and then returned to get his own food.

"So?" he asked after she'd taken her first bite.

"It's good. But..." She leaned forward. "As you said, it's breakfast food."

He laughed. "Even Chris can cook a few eggs and bacon."

"Yes, Chris, I fear, has taken after my father in the kitchen. My father once almost burned down our house when he tried to reheat a slice of pizza in the toaster. He had a bright idea that if he turned the toaster on its side, it would work just fine."

"I've actually seen Chris do that very same thing." Eric shook his head as he chuckled.

"So, I was thinking we could take that walk after breakfast. Not that it's stopped snowing, but..." She shrugged. "I think if we add a few layers of clothing we'll be okay."

"Sounds good. Somehow the short walk I took last night was more exhilarating than cold," he replied.

"Then it's settled." She nodded and finished her breakfast.

"Too bad it's not a bright sunny day. We could pack a picnic lunch and enjoy the beach for a few hours."

"If it was a bright sunny day, then we wouldn't be here. We'd be in Portland by now," she pointed out. Instantly, she noticed the change in him. He sobered a little before nodding once.

"It would have been a shame. Not seeing this place." He looked around. "I've added it to my visit-again list."

She had too. She wanted to see the view in the spring or summer. And she'd been dreaming of a day on the beach. Since moving to California, she'd only had a few days where she'd escaped to spend time in the sun.

"I'd like to see it in the summer," she agreed.

"Well, it's definitely not summer out there now, but it is beautiful." He finished his breakfast. "I'll do the dishes while you layer up." He smiled and took her empty plate and glass.

Disappearing into her room, she pulled a pair of jeans over the yoga pants, then took her wool socks out of her bag and put them on. After two tries, she managed to pull on her Uggs. She desperately wished for the snow boots that she'd left at her parents' house. She hadn't believed she would need them in Cali. She pulled off her sweatshirt and put on a tank top and a T-shirt, before putting the sweatshirt back on.

She pulled on a beanie, grabbed a scarf, and headed back out.

Eric was already there, waiting for her, his jacket and scarf in hand.

"Think you'll be warm enough?" he asked, assessing her outfit.

"I'm breaking a sweat now," she joked, opening the

door. Taking a deep breath, she almost choked as the frigid air closed her throat.

Eric was there, gently slapping her on the back until she caught her breath.

"Jesus, it's freezing out here." She wrapped her arms around herself.

"Change your mind?" he asked, shutting the door to the cabin behind him.

Looking around, she saw the beauty surrounding them and wanted to explore. "No," she said after a moment. She took Eric's hand and started pulling him down the cleared pathway towards the sand.

When they hit the beach, it was hard to tell where the sand ended and the snow started. There was a slight breeze blowing, which had the white powder mixing with the darker sand.

They remained in silence as they crossed the expanse of the sand. Stopping a few feet away from the water's edge, they watched the waves break, clearing the snow from the sand as soon as it landed.

"I've never been on the beach when it's snowing before," she said.

"I hadn't either. There's something…"

"Mesmerizing about it all," she finished for him. She was more aware now than before that he hadn't dropped her hand. Even though they were both wearing gloves, she felt the heat rush through his hand into her own.

"I thought it was magical being in the city for Christmas, but this…" He shook his head.

"Yeah," she agreed as they started walking down the beach. "So," she said after a few feet, "what did Chris say?"

"About?" he asked, looking at her sideways.

She motioned to their joined hands. "This."

He sighed and glanced out over the water, and she could tell he was trying to avoid the conversation.

She knew the moment that he'd mentioned he'd talked to Chris that he'd told her brother about their kiss. The two of them had remained close all of these years. She'd had friends come and go during her school years. None of them had stuck like Eric and Chris had.

She knew that they didn't keep secrets from one another. Ever. Once, her brother's girlfriend had tried to hit on Eric at a party. By the time the party had closed down, Chris had broken up with the girl and it was all over the school that it was because of what had happened.

Tugging his hand, she pulled him to a stop and took a slight step closer to him. She searched his eyes.

"No matter what he said, it won't change the way I feel, the way I've always felt about you." She waited, biting her lip as the seconds ticked by.

CHAPTER 8

What was he supposed to do with that? He'd waited years to have a chance with Alice. Now his best friend had pretty much signed off on letting him take that chance.

Not to mention, here she was, practically throwing herself directly in front of him. He wanted her. Period. But there was the voice in his head screaming for him to be careful. This would mean more to him than any other relationship had or ever would. After all, if by chance their relationship didn't last, his and Chris's would go on.

He ran his hands up and down her arms and then pulled her close until her head rested on his shoulder. "Promise me," he said against her forehead.

"Anything." She wrapped her arms around his waist.

"No matter what happens, we remain friends."

She chuckled. "I can't make that promise." She leaned back and looked into his eyes. "Let's say you decide to cheat on me with Lisa Carver…"

"Who?" He frowned.

"Chris's ex, the one who…"

"Oh," he interrupted her and chuckled. "Right. Trust me, that isn't an issue."

"Or a Lisa Carver type." She ran her hands up his sides. "Then, I'm afraid, I'd have to cut your heart out." She leaned up on her toes and kissed him. "I take it that my brother has given you his approval finally."

He sighed, enjoying the feeling of her lips on his. "Sort of," he agreed. "That doesn't mean that I'm going to jump you the first chance I get."

"Why not?" she asked, pulling herself closer. "You can't tell me you don't want to."

No, he couldn't. He couldn't even say that he hadn't thought about doing just that when she'd walked out that morning in that thin tank top.

"What I want and what I should do are two different things." His eyes moved to her lips. "Like, right now, I want to drag you down into the soft sand and kiss you until neither of us can see straight."

She chuckled. "Why don't you?"

"Because it's easily below ten degrees out here and we'd get soaking wet, not to mention I'd want to remove some of those layers you have on." His hands moved to just under her shirt, touching her skin. He felt her shiver when the wind snuck under her clothes.

"Okay, good point," she said, wiggling free of him and pulling her shirts back into place. "How about we go in, have another cup of hot chocolate, and build a really hot fire?"

"Now I could go for that." He took her hand and they started walking back across the beach. The snow had picked up and was now falling in even larger clumps. The wind had grown stronger as well and by the time they hit the mouth of the pathway, he was gripping her hand tightly.

"I don't think I can feel my toes." She laughed as she stomped the snow from her Uggs on the covered front porch. He shook the snow from himself and opened the door.

He'd left the embers burning in the fireplace and welcomed the warmth as they shut themselves inside again.

Their extra layers disappeared quickly, and he tossed a few logs on the fire while she made them each a hot chocolate.

By the time the fire was roaring again, they each had a cup in their hands as they sat on the sofa in front of the fire. He'd pulled the blanket around her shoulders again.

"What did my brother really say?" she asked once she was settled.

He thought about it for a moment. He'd never really lied to Chris. They had come up with a code a few years after claiming they were officially best friends. He'd lived up to that code and was pretty sure Chris had as well. Mutual respect, which he also had for Alice. He'd never lied to her before and had no intention of starting.

"He pretty much said that we had his blessings." He sipped his drink.

"Really?" She turned slightly to him.

"What did you expect him to do?" he asked, knowing full well that he'd believed that Chris would disown him as a friend after punching him a few times.

She shrugged and set her cup down. "I don't know, maybe threaten to hit you?"

He chuckled. "My thoughts exactly. But he shocked us both and told me it was about time."

Her eyebrows shot up. "He said that?" Eric nodded and set his own mug aside.

They remained silent for a moment, watching the fire lap at the new logs. "This is nice." She sighed and leaned against his shoulder. Automatically, his arm went around her and pulled her closer to him.

"Yes," he agreed, feeling nervous all of a sudden. His desire for her had been so strong over the years. He'd had plenty of fantasies about what it would be like being with her. Touching her. Kissing her. Making love to her.

None of those fantasies had been in front of a fireplace when they were trapped in a snowstorm.

He glanced down at her as she looked up at him. Their eyes locked and just as he was leaning closer to taste that sweet mouth of hers once more, there was a knock on the door.

Sighing, he got up from the sofa and opened the door.

Todd Jordan stood on the other side, a bundle of chopped wood in his arms. "Morning." He smiled. "I was just checking in to see if you needed anything?"

"No," he said, eager to get back to Alice.

"Good." Todd nodded. "I've brought you guys some more wood." He motioned to the armload. "I'll bring the rest up and leave it here." He motioned to the wood stack that Eric had been getting the wood from.

"Sure," he said.

"Looks like you two enjoyed a walk on the beach." Todd motioned towards the wet boots they had left sitting outside.

"Yes." He smiled.

"Just a tip—you might want to bring the boots inside. We have a few young dogs and they like to chew on boots." He motioned to his own worn boots. One of them had teeth marks in the top of them.

Eric laughed. "What kind of dogs?" he asked as Todd set the logs down and moved to get the rest.

"A lab mix and a mutt." He laughed. "No matter what I do, both of them love the taste of feet."

Eric leaned against the doorjamb. "My folks had a lab mix with the same issue. Apple cider vinegar. Just spray it on your shoes a few times and make sure there are plenty of treats around."

"I've tried that. In the house it works like a charm," Todd said putting down the next load from the wheelbarrow. "It's a lot harder to spray on the shoes our customers leave outside. Hence the warning." He smiled.

"I'll move them in." He bent and set the shoes inside, thankful that they appeared unharmed.

"Thanks. The boys sure do love playing in the snow." He wiped his forehead with a handkerchief. "With our third baby due any day now, I've been so busy getting things ready, I've neglected training them." He sighed.

"Wow, three kids?" Eric smiled. "Boys? Girls?"

"One of each so far," Todd answered proudly.

"What is this one?" he asked.

We're hoping for a boy, but my sister swears it will be a girl."

"You don't know? I thought everyone always found out?"

"Megan likes surprises." He smiled. "I'll let you get back inside." Todd nodded to where Alice was sitting on the sofa, watching them. “Have a good day. Remember, if you want, dinner is up at the main house.”

“Thanks,” Eric said before shutting the door.

“Three kids,” Alice repeated once he sat back down next to her.

“Yeah.” He looked at her sideways. “What’s wrong with three?”

“Oh, nothing.” She smiled. “I was just…”

“What?” he asked when she didn’t finish.

She looked him directly in the eyes and shocked him by saying, “I was just imagining what my children would look like.”

CHAPTER 9

She held her breath as she waited for him to respond. Here she was, moments away from finally getting what she'd waited her entire life for with him, and she was pouring out the rest of her heart.

What would she do if he laughed at her? She couldn't imagine being stuck in a small cabin if he turned her away because she had dreams.

"I was thinking the same thing," he said softly. "Well, I mean, I think that everyone dreams about it at one point or another. Don't you?"

She nodded as he moved closer to her. "Yes." It came out as a whisper.

"But I'm not quite ready for kids, yet." His eyes moved to her lips.

"Me either." She smiled. "Besides, my father would kill me if I told him I was pregnant." She'd meant it as a joke but seeing the look on Eric's face had her mentally kicking herself.

"For a moment, I'd forgotten about your dad," he said

with a slight frown.

She hadn't meant to bring her family into the mix. "Eric," she started, but he shook his head.

"No, don't." He stood up. "I… have to make a call."

"To who?" She gasped. "Not my father?" She jumped up from the sofa. "He has nothing—"

"No." His chuckle stopped her. "Not your father."

"Who then?" she asked.

"Your mother."

"Why would you call my mother?" She crossed her arms over her chest.

"Because, I made a promise…" He shook his head. "Just because."

Her eyes narrowed as she glared at him. "Why?"

He sighed. "Alice, Jane is like my second mom. She had me promise that if there was ever a chance that we…"—he motioned between them—"that I'd…" He pushed his hands through his hair. "Never mind."

"No." She drew the word out and waved at him. "Please, go on. I'd like to hear how you promised my mother"—her voice spiked slightly at the word—"that you'd call or… text her if you and I ever hooked up."

"It's not…" He shook his head and she could tell he was frustrated. "It's just… She was going to…"

"What?" she asked, her temper flaring now.

"Play defense and take the heat and try to break it to your dad as gently as possible," he finished, looking even more frustrated.

"So, my mom… knew?" she asked, unsure.

"Sort of." He shrugged. "I guess."

"When?" she asked, feeling the heat of the room cause her face to flush. Or maybe it was the fact that her mother had assumed that one day they would end up like this. Together.

Eric avoided looking at her and she moved closer.

"Eric?"

"Graduation," he blurted out.

"Yours or mine?" she asked remembering both parties.

"Mine," he answered quickly.

"My mother knew…" She tried to not let her jaw fall at the thought of her mother guessing so long ago.

Eric just shrugged again and backed another step away from her. She closed the gap instantly.

"My family," she started as she wrapped her arms around his shoulders, "has nothing to do with us. Even though my brother is your best friend, my mother is practically your second mother, and my dad…" She shook her head. "Let's not think about my dad."

"Yes," he agreed quickly. "Let's not."

Before he could finish, she had plastered her body against his. "Let's not think about any of my family members." She leaned up and touched her lips softly to his. It was amazing that the spark she'd felt the first time jumped through her again.

Then his hands rested on her hips and pulled her closer and the spark turned into a full-blown fire raging through every ounce of her, reaching down deep into her core.

"Eric." She didn't recognize her own voice. It was deeper and vibrated from her chest.

"Alice." He hoisted her up into his arms, and she'd never felt anything like being held by him. "I never thought…" He shook his head as he walked towards the bedrooms. "I'd dreamed." He kissed her again. "Don't let this be a dream," he said as he stepped into his bedroom.

"No." She smiled. "It's not." She reached over and smiled as she pinched his shoulder.

"Okay." He laughed. "Not a dream." He set her down slowly on her feet again and held onto her as his mouth covered hers once more.

When she felt her body falling backward, she held onto him as he lowered them both to the bed.

"I'm going to go slow," he said, his mouth just under her ear. His hot breath caused goosebumps on her skin, and she arched so he could trail his mouth lower.

"Yes," she sighed and gripped his shoulders. She would have agreed to anything, knowing it was Eric who was running his hands over her, his mouth over her skin.

She felt his fingers nudge her shirt up, exposing the tank top. Before pulling that aside, she thought she heard him curse.

"You've got layers too." She reached for his shirt and, before he could remove hers, he had it over his head and on the floor.

She watched him as he leaned back and slowly nudged both her shirt and tank over her head.

"Alice." Her name was just a whisper. "You're even more beautiful than I imagined."

She chuckled. "You've seen me in a swimsuit before." She reached for her bra, but he stopped her.

"No, let me. When I'm ready." He came back down to her, his arms on either side of her body as he hovered over her, kissing her.

She felt her body begin to shake as his free hand roamed up her ribs, over her flat belly, then back up to cup her through her silky bra.

"You make me so…" His mouth left hers and then

started trailing kisses down her shoulder and over her bra until he finally settled and sucked her nipple through the silk.

Her fingers went to his thick hair, holding him as he caused her entire body to shake even more.

She could feel herself growing wet. She had never waited this long for anything in her life.

"Eric, I want..." She shook her head. "No, I need..." she corrected herself.

His hand shifted to the clasp of her jeans. When he started to tug, she realized that her yoga pants would have to be taken off as well.

Reaching a hand down, she helped him remove both layers.

"Socks," she said, eagerly.

"It's like unwrapping a Christmas present," he said. He chuckled when her yoga pants got stuck on her thick wool socks.

She smiled and wished that they were someplace tropical and all she was wearing was a string bikini instead.

When she reached for his pants, he pulled away and stood next to the bed. Yanking them off his legs quickly, he stood at the foot of the bed in nothing but boxer briefs, looking sexier than she'd remembered.

Eric and her brother were gym buddies as well. The duo worked out on a regular basis, which meant his thighs were thicker than her waist. She smiled, anxious to feel him next to her again.

"What's that for?" he asked, remaining where he was.

"You." She ran her eyes up and down him. "I approve."

He did the same to her. "I more than approve." His

voice was a little gruff. Then he was beside her on the bed, running a fingertip from her navel to her chin. He touched the dimple next to her mouth. "This happens to be the sexiest thing on you."

She laughed. "Okay." She ran a finger down to his hips and the narrow triangle just above his boxers. "I'm particularly fond of this…" She ran a fingertip down the arrow of his hip. He sucked in his breath and closed his eyes. "Right here."

When she removed her hand, his eyes moved to her erect nipples. "These," he said softly and, with just his fingertip, touched one of them, causing them to harden even more, "are pretty high up on my list."

Not waiting, she leaned closer and cupped him. He was hard and larger than she'd experienced before.

"Eric." She swallowed, meeting his eyes with hers.

"I'm going to go slow." His smile faltered. "I swear it."

She nodded as she wrapped her arms around him and pulled him down until they were kissing again. He was so smooth. She forgot her fears moments later as he peeled her panties and bra from her heated skin.

When she lay next to him, fully naked, he again ran his eyes over her and touched her gently with just his fingertips before spreading her thighs and running a finger over her lips below. She cried out and felt her body convulsing.

"Yes," he begged as he slipped a finger into her, causing her to instantly lose the last of her control. "Come for me."

Nothing on earth would have made her deny him at that moment. Not Eric. She'd waited far too long and had dreamed of this very moment all of her life.

CHAPTER 10

Eric watched Alice change in front of his eyes. Gone was the young girl that had followed him around, obviously infatuated with him. She was no longer the awkward preteen with legs that were too long and braces. No, what lay before him now, in the afterglow of orgasm, was the woman of his fantasies.

Which, of course, made his cock jump and grow even more painfully hard.

While she lay there on the comforter, breathing hard from the release, he reached into the nightstand, thankful he'd packed a box of condoms for the trip, and slid one on.

When he moved above her, her eyes slid open, a smile of pure satisfaction on her lips as she gripped his hips and spread her legs wide to take him in.

"This means something," he said, unsure of why he needed to do so.

"Yes," she said softly and pulled him down until their lips met. When he slid slowly into her, he couldn't stop a moan of pure joy from vibrating from his chest.

"My god," he whispered once he was fully embedded into her.

"I need…" She bit her bottom lip and dug her nails into his skin. "Move, I need…"

He chuckled, trying to keep a little control, but then she jerked her hips up closer to him, and he could have sworn his eyes crossed as pure euphoria spread throughout his entire being.

Suddenly, he couldn't control himself as he moved over her, in her. She surrounded him more than he'd ever imagined. Her arms, her legs, her pussy. Everything she was, held him as if she was made to embrace him.

He lost track of time as sweat rolled down his back as they moved as one. He felt her second release and growled moments later with his own.

He fell breathlessly onto her after his entire body gave out, knowing there was nothing left to give and not caring at all.

"Eric," she grunted a few minutes later. "You're heavier than you look."

He chuckled and rolled until he lay beside her, holding her tightly in his arms.

"Better?" he asked.

"Much." She sighed and rested her head on his shoulder. "This was better than my beach fantasy," she said out of the blue.

Chuckling again, he glanced down at her. "This beach? With snow and all?"

"No." She laughed. "Someplace tropical. Warm." She sighed. "Where I was wearing nothing but a string bikini and you were…"

"You need not go any further." He stopped her. "I'm in."

She laughed as he ran his hands over her hips. "The last time I saw you in a bathing suit, Chris about punched me."

She leaned up until she was looking down at him. "When was that?"

"Last Fourth of July." He suddenly felt hungry.

"Fourth…" She frowned down at him. "You didn't make it to that party."

He remembered too late. "I did." He cringed. "But after I saw you, and your brother saw me seeing you…" He sighed. "I left."

"You… left?" She shook her head. "Why?"

He sat up and sat on the edge of the bed, reaching down to pull on his boxers.

"Eric?" she asked, moving over to the side of the bed with him. The fact that she was still completely naked didn't go unnoticed by him.

He turned and, trying to keep his eyes on her face, said, "Because I knew then that there was no way I would be able to keep my hands off of you that day."

Not waiting for her to respond, he got off the bed and walked into the next room.

When she joined him, she had pulled on those tight yoga pants and the tank top, sans the bra underneath. Her nipples were still very hard and poked through the light material, causing his eyes to focus only on them.

"Up here, pretty boy," she purred as she walked towards him. When her fingertips nudged his chin up until their eyes met, he realized he'd been practically drooling. "Did you really leave the beach party because of that?"

He nodded, not trusting his voice. He needed a glass of water to cool off. No, hell, he needed a beer. Already he could feel himself growing harder.

She watched his reaction as she reached down and touched his boxers, rubbing the soft material over his hard-on until he closed his eyes and leaned into her.

"And now?" she asked. He shook his head, not understanding the question.

"Why aren't your hands on me now?" she asked. He jerked the moment the question was out, taking her in his arms and plastering her against the counter. Her pinned her between him and the microwave as his mouth crushed hers and his hands jerked the yoga pants down her hips.

This time, he wasn't going to go slow and wait. This time, when he pushed his finger into her heat, she cried out his name and he reveled in the sound of excitement from her lips.

She kicked off the yoga pants and spread her legs wide so he could slide between her thighs. In one quick motion he was inside her while her legs wrapped around his hips and her arms around him.

She cried out his name over and over as he pounded into her blindly. "I can't…" He shook his head. "I can't wait."

"No, don't. I'm…" She arched and fell at the same time he did.

Eric didn't like the fact that his legs were made of jelly or that his shorts were around his ankles. But when he realized he'd just come in Alice without a condom, he froze.

"Oh my god," he said slowly. "I…" He jerked away from her as if he'd been burned.

"What?" Her eyes opened quickly, looking around the

room. "What?" she said again when he just stared at her blankly.

"I was in a hurry. I… forgot…" He swallowed.

When she started laughing, he cursed.

"It's okay," she said between giggles. "I've been on the pill since… well, a long time, and I'm never late taking them."

He relaxed a little. "I'm clean. I have a yearly…"

"Eric, it's me." She jumped from the counter as he pulled up his shorts. "I know you are." She moved over and kissed him. "I'm the same. My checkup is every birthday month, which was…"

"Two months ago," he answered for her, causing her to smile.

"Right." She kissed him. "Now I'm going to make some soup and turkey sandwiches. I'm starving."

They sat in front of the fire and ate, telling each other what they each liked most about the holidays.

It was easy for him—being with family. His or hers. He'd spent as many holidays around her family as he had his own. He supposed that their mothers being best friends from high school had something to do with it. Still, after his folks had moved, he had to admit things had been hard. He'd felt like his time was split between the two families, and he was having to choose where he ended up.

This year it had been easy after Chris had asked him to drive Alice home. He'd called his sister and brothers and told them all that he'd be coming back to Portland this year instead of heading down to Arizona with his folks.

"It's hard on my mother," she said after they had finished their food. "Your mom being so far away. My mother is actually thinking of buying a place in Arizona."

"Really?" he asked. She'd snuggled up next to him and they were both watching the fire and the snow, which continued to fall heavily outside.

"Yes." She sighed. "Which wouldn't be as hard on me and Chris as it was on your siblings."

"My sister and brothers complain a lot about having their kids' grandparents so far away," he agreed.

"Do you think they'll move back?" she asked, glancing up at him.

"I doubt it. Dad's health…" He immediately stopped talking.

"What?" Alice sat up and looked at him. "What about your dad?"

Shaking his head, he closed his eyes. "I wasn't supposed to tell you, since it will probably get back to your mother, who will worry." He relayed his mother's fears, even though he'd promised more than a dozen times he wouldn't say anything, even to Chris.

"Eric." She narrowed her eyes at him. "What?"

"He's been really low on vitamin D along with a few other things. His asthma had gotten really bad in the past few years."

"Yes, I'd heard that was why they moved away." She leaned back against him, his arms going back around her. He enjoyed the way her body fit against his, so soft as her sexy scent surrounded him.

"Well, he had a really bad asthma attack and they were thinking of putting him on oxygen full time."

"I didn't know that."

"No." He shook his head. "No one does. My father didn't want anyone to know, so after some advice from some more doctors… they moved." He shrugged.

"How's he doing now?" she asked.

"Much better." He smiled remembering how his father's latest tests had come back in the clear. He pulled her closer and sighed, wishing for a nap.

"I know we talked about playing board games, but I don't want to move from this spot."

"Me either." She sighed and tucked her feet up on the sofa. "Do you think it's going to stop snowing soon?"

He was quiet for a while, then answered, "I hope not."

CHAPTER 11

The sound of her cell phone ringing woke Alice from her nap. She usually hated napping, but lying here snuggled next to Eric, she wished they didn't have to move for the rest of the day.

Groaning, she started to get up to go find it.

"Leave it." He sighed and pulled her closer. "It will go to voicemail." The cabin grew silent again. "See." He shifted and was suddenly hovering above her, his lips gently brushing across hers.

"It could have been important," she suggested as his mouth lowered and trailed down her neck.

"If it was, they'd call back." He leaned up and waited a moment for the ringing to start again. "Nope, not important." He returned to kissing her.

She could just imagine spending the rest of the week just like this, wrapped in his arms as the snow fell and the world outside the windows stopped. This time when they came together, she allowed herself to cut loose and really enjoy going slow. Running her hands over him after, as they lay in front of the fireplace naked, she explored every little scar he had, remembering where he'd gotten a few.

"Where did you get this one?" she asked, running her finger over a small star-shaped scar just over his ribs on the left.

He glanced down and chuckled. "Barbed wire fence. Chris dared me to try and dive between the wires." He was running his hands through her hair. "Stupid me, I took a running start and…" He shrugged. "Got a new scar for the trouble."

She giggled. "When was that?"

"Last week," he said soberly, causing her to laugh even more. "I think we were ten."

She smiled and rested her chin on his chest. "You were so handsome when you were ten."

His dark eyebrows shot up. "I'm not now?"

"You are." She smiled. "But I was eight when I noticed you for the first time."

"Noticed?"

"You know, noticed, noticed." She felt her face heat.

"Really? What was it that my ten-year-old self had that drew your eye?"

She smiled and thought about it. "Dark eyes, a slight dimple here." She reached up and touched his cheek. "And you helped me when I fell."

"Chivalry isn't dead." He pulled her closer.

"At least it wasn't for ten-year-old you," she said between kisses.

He pulled the blanket over them when she shivered.

"I'm getting hungry again," he admitted after a while.

"Me too."

"I was thinking that homemade meal that Todd was talking about sounded pretty good."

She leaned up and looked out the window. The snow had slowed down a lot. "We have just enough time to shower." She got up, taking the blanket with her, leaving him on the rug in front of the fire completely naked. "Too bad I'm not a painter," she joked as she looked down at him. "You'd make a great model."

"I've modeled naked before," he said, standing up and following her into the bathroom. "Actually, that's how Chris and I paid for a trip to Mexico last summer."

She laughed. "Somehow, I'm not surprised."

After a long hot shower that filled the small bathroom with steam, she disappeared into her own room and pulled on a pair of warm black pants and the red sweater that she had bought to wear on Christmas morning. Once the bathroom was clear of fog, she dried her hair and applied her makeup.

When she walked out into the living area, Chris was just getting off the phone.

"It looks like…" he started to say before turning around. "Wow, you look amazing." His eyes ran over her.

"Thanks." She smiled.

"It looks like your brother and Dawn are going to jump on a flight to Atlanta tomorrow since this storm is supposed to pick up again late tonight."

"How much more of the stuff can fall?" she asked, looking outside now.

The pathway was still cleared, probably thanks to Todd, but everywhere else, the snow was piled high. She couldn't even see the bench at the entrance of the beach path anymore. Instead, there was just a mound of white snow.

"They say at least double this before Christmas morning."

His words sunk in. "We're going to be stuck here for Christmas?" she asked, feeling her heart sink slightly.

She'd dreamed of being stuck with him like this, but in those dreams, she'd still made it home to spend the holiday with her parents.

"It looks like it." He walked over to her. "Would it be so bad spending Christmas here with me?"

"No." She turned around and wrapped her arms around his neck. "Of course not. It's just…"

"You won't get any presents?" he joked, causing her to smile.

"No, that's not it. I was hoping to see my family during my break."

"You still might be able to."

"No, I only have two weeks off."

"From school?" He frowned. "But I thought…"

"No." She turned to him. "I've been interning at a local clinic."

"When did you start that?" he asked, taking her coat from the rack and helping her pull it on.

"Earlier this year," she replied, remembering when she'd first started helping out at the local VA hospital. At that point, she hadn't decided on a career yet. Now, after spending some time with the wounded military men and women that she helped on a weekly basis, she had. "It's making me lean towards becoming a physical therapist. I still haven't decided for good, but…"

"That's great," he said, pulling on his own coat. "I'll

bet that you're already good at it." He turned towards the door and then glanced back at her. "Ready for the cold?"

She wrapped her scarf around her shoulders and her face and then nodded. "Let's do this," she said, causing him to chuckle.

They rushed down the cleared pathway, hand in hand. Eric helped her when she slipped a few times on the ice. Her Uggs just weren't built for this much snow or ice.

By the time they reached the front porch of the big house, they were both a little breathless. The place was lit up with Christmas lights everywhere, putting her even more in the holiday spirit.

"Wow, this place is amazing," she whispered.

There was a little sign hanging just above the doorbell.

"Come on in, wipe your feet, and don't mind the dogs."

"Do you think they have one that says, 'Go away, we'd like some privacy'?" Eric joked softly as they walked in, causing her to chuckle.

The entryway was all decked out in lights and a huge Christmas tree sat near the base of a beautiful staircase.

"Back here," a woman called out cheerfully. They followed the voices and stepped into a large dining room filled with people.

Todd Jordan stood up from his spot next to a young boy who looked just like him and a little blonde girl in a highchair. A very pregnant blonde woman sat at the head of the table, smiling at them.

"You must be Eric and Alice. I'm Megan. Todd was telling me a little about the two of you." She motioned for them to take the empty chairs at the long table. "Of course, if he'd let me get out of the house once in a while, I could have met the both of you when you arrived," she said under her breath.

Todd chuckled. "You're free to come and go, after the snowstorm."

Megan reached over and took her husband's hand in hers. "I slipped once," she informed the table. "It was more of a trip than anything." She rubbed her free hand over her large belly.

"You face-planted in the bushes," Todd corrected her. Megan chuckled.

"Please." Megan motioned to the food. "Help yourself." Food was passed around as they dished up homemade meatloaf, mashed potatoes, and beans.

"Are you two enjoying your stay?" a young Asian woman asked from down the table.

"Yes, very much so," Alice answered.

"Where are you from?" the woman asked.

"Portland. You two? I hear… New Orleans?" she guessed.

"Yes." The woman's eyebrows shot up. "Born and raised." The woman looked over to her husband, a thin black man who looked too busy enjoying the food to chat. "Charles and I both."

"What brings you to Portland?" Eric asked the other couple. He was trying not to focus on how cute the kids were and how he'd instantly thought about having kids with Alice upon seeing them.

"We wished to see snow for Christmas," the woman answered easily.

"Well, you definitely got your wish," Todd added with a chuckle. "We're supposed to get even more tonight.

After dinner I'll drop off more firewood and clear the path again."

"It's all been so wonderful," Alice started. "We're just so thankful we stopped here instead of somewhere along I-five."

"Yes." He thought about being stuck at a highway hotel and cringed. "I doubt they'd have meatloaf this good anywhere else."

"Not to mention having our own cabin," Alice added.

"How long have you two been married?" Charles asked.

"Oh, we're—"

Alice grabbed his hand, stopping him.

"We've known each since I was five and he was seven," she answered truthfully. She'd booked the cabin under his name, but it wasn't her fault that Megan had assumed they were married. Why not let the little fantasy week play out.

"Oh, childhood sweethearts," Charles' wife said with a sigh. "It shows. You two are so in tune with one another."

Alice looked at him with a smile. "Yes, we are."

CHAPTER 12

The following two days they spent pretty much the same way. Each day they ventured out into the thick snow that surrounded them, then enjoyed breakfast, lunch, and a nap before heading to the big house for dinner with the others. And, more importantly, each night they spent wrapped in each other's arms, making love slowly in front of the fireplace as the snow continued to build outside.

Alice talked to her family and he talked to his. The storm was making national news as one of the worst storms in the history of the West Coast. It spread far beyond the little area they were trapped in and threatened to continue past the holidays and possibly even into the New Year.

At this point, neither of them really cared anymore. They were in their own fantasy snow-globe world.

It was magical and suited all their needs. Of course, in a few days when their own supplies started to run low, they might need to venture out further. Todd had mentioned to him that his family was heading into town the following evening for a special town event and to restock their own supplies and could easily take them with him.

Alice had hinted that she would enjoy heading into town when he suggested going along.

"Did they mention what the town event was?" she asked.

"No, just that he was taking the entire family in and that they had plenty of room for us to join them."

They were lying in bed, wrapped in the warm blankets, their bodies cooling from their recent lovemaking.

Oddly, even though he was tired, his mind was going too quickly to fall asleep anytime soon. He could tell Alice was already falling asleep, since she was slightly slurring her words and every now and then a yawn escaped.

"What would you think about staying in Portland for a while? Would it be possible?"

"Sure." She sighed, and he could tell that she had fallen asleep.

He waited almost a half hour before untangling himself from her. Pulling on his sweats and a shirt, he moved into the living room and turned on his laptop for the first time.

He found the email he'd received last week from his father's friend and read it a few times. The job offer was a once-in-a-lifetime opportunity. One that, last week, he'd easily brushed aside. Now, however, he thought about creating something more solid, building something better with Alice.

He created a draft email accepting the offer but held off on hitting send until after he could talk to Alice.

When he crawled back in bed next to her, she automatically turned to him in her sleep, snuggling into his chest.

Wrapping his arms around her, he closed his eyes, enjoying the way her body fit against his.

The next morning, he cooked the rest of their eggs. They had finished off all of the bacon the day before, so he pulled out a few slices of turkey, diced them up, and put them in the eggs. There were only three slices of bread left for toast, but they had a box of blueberry muffins. He poured the rest of the orange juice into glasses just as Alice walked out of the bathroom.

"It's a good thing we're heading into town today." She smiled as she sat down.

"It's not the Ritz, but at least we have all of this left." He motioned to the box of muffins.

"Good thing you grabbed two boxes. We'll have to get a lot more supplies this time, since we know we'll be stuck here for a while longer."

"Yeah, I've already made a list." He motioned to the small tablet.

She laughed. "I had almost forgotten you were a list kind of guy."

He smiled across at her. "I had forgotten that you weren't."

She shrugged. "There's probably lots we don't have in common," she said between bites. "Like, you're a summer person and I'm a winter."

"No." He shook his head after thinking about it. "I think now"—his eyes met hers—"I like winter just fine."

She smiled and he felt his heart skip. She'd always done that to him, but now he knew there wasn't anything standing between them.

"Okay, you hate school. I love it," she added.

He sobered. "Right." He hadn't thought about her

education when he'd been planning last night. Now he did as she continued to list off a few other small things that they didn't have in common.

"You're not listening to me," she said after a moment.

"Sure, I am," he lied. Her eyebrows shot up.

"Oh?" She leaned closer. "Then what was the last thing I said?"

"You like cats and I like dogs," he pulled from his memory.

"No, I said that like five minutes ago." She leaned back and chuckled. "Where did you go?"

"Portland," he answered honestly.

"Okay, I'll bite. Why?"

"I had an offer." He stood up and took the empty dishes to the sink.

"What kind of offer?" she asked following him.

"A job offer. One from my dad's old buddy at the Krieger plant."

"That's great." The excitement in her voice told him that she hadn't thought it through yet.

"It's in Portland," he said, turning towards her, leaving the dirty dishes in the sink.

"And?" She waited.

"And you're heading back to Cali to finish school," he supplied. She actually shrank a little. Her shoulders slumped and she frowned, getting the cute little crease between her brows she normally had when she was deep in thought.

"So, we've waited this long…" She bit her bottom lip.

He took her shoulders in his hands and pulled her close. "Right," he said, instead of talking her into it. "If that's what you want." He kissed the top of her head and, before she could see the sadness in his eyes, turned back towards the sink to wash the dishes.

He heard her leave the room and closed his eyes as he leaned on the counter. Clearing his mind, he finished the dishes and decided he needed a quick walk.

He knocked on her bedroom door and could hear her talking to someone. When she opened the door, she was holding the phone to her shoulder.

"I'm going to take a walk," he told her, then he motioned to her phone. "Sorry."

"It's okay." She smiled. "Stay warm."

He turned and left. Hitting the trail, he headed towards the beach. He was a little surprised when he found a woman walking towards him, two dogs on her heels.

"Morning." She smiled at him and instantly he guessed that the woman was related to Todd.

"Morning." He smiled back.

"I'm Lacey, Todd's sister. My husband and I live just…" She motioned towards a hill. "Over there."

"Eric Jenkins," he replied. "We're staying in the end cabin."

"Oh, you're the couple that got stuck on the trip up to Portland. Megan was telling me about how nice the two of you are. You and your wife."

He smiled and nodded, but the woman's eyes ran over his face.

"Oh my god," she said, startling him, "you're not really married, are you?"

He was taken back. "How… How did you know?"

"I have my ways." She smiled. "But you've known each other forever," she said as he bent to pet one of the dogs.

"Yes." He sighed. "Her brother is my best friend."

"How romantic." Lacey chuckled.

"Yeah, until now, we've been… like brother and sister." He straightened, but the other dog had waddled up and was now demanding attention.

"Nothing like being stuck in a snowstorm to strip away those layers." Lacey smiled. "Sounds like you need some time alone to think." She motioned towards the beach. "You couldn't ask for a better spot to do it. Even if there is two feet of snow on the ground."

"Yeah, I'm already planning on making a trip back here in the summer."

"You'll fall in love with the town." She smiled. "Come on Bo and JoJo, let's leave the man alone. He needs to figure out how to convince his best friends' sister to marry him." She laughed as she started walking down the path towards her brother's house.

"How did…" he said to her back, but he was greeted with another laugh.

"It was nice meeting you, Eric Jenkins. Oh, and welcome to Pride," she called out.

CHAPTER 13

Alice sat between the two car seats in the back of the full-sized truck and enjoyed the short drive into town.

She'd given Eric the seat up front next to Megan since there was more legroom.

"It's a good thing I put the chains on this thing last week," Todd said as they pulled into town. "I'm not sure how many others from town will make it in for this thing, but at least I know my brothers' and sister's families have made it here." He nodded to a few other trucks.

"I met your sister today," Eric told Todd.

"You did?" Todd chuckled. "Don't let her spook you. She's just… that way."

Eric hadn't mentioned to her that he'd met anyone on his walk earlier.

"What way?" she asked from the back seat.

"Lacey has a gift. My grandmother, if she was alive, would have believed that she could see into people."

"Oh?" Eric asked. His voice sounded a little off.

"What did she say to you?" Alice asked.

"Nothing." He glanced over his shoulder towards her. "Just… welcome to Pride," he answered as Todd turned off the truck. They had parked across from the grocery store, but she could just see the town square out the window and gasped.

The little area where the Christmas lights and trees were last time was filled with people all dressed in holiday cheer. There were tables where people were handing out hot drinks and a huge bonfire in the middle with several smaller ones scattered around. People gathered around each one, trying to stay warm as the snow continued to fall.

"It's the official Christmas town hall lighting," Megan said as she started to get her son out of the car. Todd rushed over and nudged her aside and took his son, setting him down in the snow. "I've got Sara, you take Matt and head on over to get warm." He waved his wife away as he reached for his sleepy daughter in her car seat.

"Official?" Alice asked. "Aren't the lights already lit?"

Todd chuckled in response. "You'll see." He shifted his daughter in his arms so he could grab the thick blanket and toss it over her sleeping body.

"Come on, I'll introduce you to the rest of our family." He motioned.

Eric walked over and took her hand. "Well, you wanted to come along." He nudged her. "This looks amazing," he said softly.

"Yeah," she agreed. "Who does this sort of thing anymore? Especially in a major snowstorm?"

"Apparently, Pride does," he said as they caught up with Todd.

For the next half hour, they were introduced to a few people, including Todd and Lacey's younger brother, Iian, who was deaf. They met his wife, Allison, who, they were shocked to find out, was one of Alice's favorite artists. She even had a print of one of the woman's pieces hanging above her bed in her dorm room.

They also met Lacey's husband, Aaron, who was the town doctor. They had a daughter who was fast asleep in a stroller.

There was a loud whistle and everyone's attention turned towards an older gray-haired man.

"That's the mayor," Lacey said over her shoulder.

"We all thought you were the mayor of Pride," Todd said under his breath, earning him a poke in the ribs from Lacey.

"Shh," she said as the mayor started to speak.

"Welcome to Pride's annual town hall Christmas lighting. I'm especially pleased that everyone could make it in such beautiful weather." There were a lot of chuckles from the crowd. "Now, I know everyone's cold and tired and probably wanting to get back home to their warm houses, so I'll make this short…"

"That would be a first," someone shouted from the crowd, causing more laughter to erupt.

"Okay." The mayor chuckled. "I just have to thank a few people"—there were a few groans—"without whom this beautiful display wouldn't have been possible." A few cheers. "To the Jordan family, your consistent support of Pride would make your father proud." There were cheers. "To Patty O'Neil." There were even more cheers. "Patty, you know exactly what you mean to this town." Everyone clapped. "And Dr. Gerard Stevens."

The crowd grew quiet. “Doc, you will be missed by many. This year, our lights are dedicated to your memory.”

There was a moment of silence, then the mayor nodded and the entire square burst into a million bright lights. She’d never seen so many in her life. Not even the malls in the city could have beat the small town’s display. The lights bounced off the crisp snow, no doubt causing a haze of light above the small town.

“I bet Santa can see us through the storm now,” Matthew Stevens said to his mother.

Alice hadn’t realized she was crying until Eric pulled her closer and wrapped his arms around her.

“Are you okay?” he asked, using his gloved fingers to wipe the tears away.

“Yes, it’s just… so amazing.” She sighed and rested her head against his chest. “I wish we could stay here forever,” she said under her breath.

“Me too,” he agreed, and they stood by the fire, looking out at the millions of lights.

When the crowd started to thin, Todd turned towards them. “We can hit the store and get those supplies now. I’ll meet you at Patty’s.” He motioned to the store just down the street a little. “I’ll get Megan and the kids settled in the truck first and then head in.”

They walked quickly towards the store. It was less than a city block away and someone had cleared all of the sidewalks, but still, they had been outside for almost an hour, and when she stepped into the store, she realized just how cold she’d gotten.

“I’ll get us a cart,” Eric said and moved over to get one.

"Did you enjoy yourselves?" Patty asked from behind the counter.

"Yes." She smiled. "I've never seen anything quite like it."

"I have some hot chocolate here. The moment the lights were flipped, I hightailed it back here. I'm too old to be standing around in the cold for too long."

Alice walked over and made two cups of hot chocolate, then handed one to Eric.

"It doesn't take age to realize you spent too much time in this cold," he said easily, causing the older woman to chuckle.

"True." She glanced over when Todd walked in. "Stocking up?" she asked them.

"Yes, we ran out of everything," Eric answered. "I guess we didn't realize that we'd be in town this long."

"From the sounds of it, you'll be enjoying Christmas with us as well," Patty called after them. "Better stock up for at least one more week."

While they walked through the aisle getting items from Eric's list, she thought of trying to find something for Eric for Christmas.

She hadn't expected to see him, but now that she knew they would be stuck here together, she wanted to have a present for him to open on Christmas morning.

Glancing out the main window, she saw a small store across the way and came up with a plan.

"I… I'd like to go across the way and get a few other… personal things." She motioned to the drug store out the front windows.

Seeing the store, Eric nodded. "I'll finish up here and meet you back at the truck."

"Thanks," she said and disappeared outside quickly.

Crossing over to the drug store, she glanced towards the windows and, instead, ducked into a small boutique, silently praying that they would have something that could pass as a gift.

She found several items and by the time she walked out, the small bag tucked deep in her purse, she noticed Todd and Eric loading the groceries into the covered bed of the truck.

"Need any help?" she asked, stopping by Eric.

"Nope, we've got this. Go ahead and jump in." Eric opened the door for her.

"Thanks." She smiled up at him and wiggled her way between the two car seats again.

The truck was warm and, this time, both kids were fast asleep.

"When are you due?" she asked Megan when they were alone. She couldn't remember if it had been mentioned at any of the dinners.

"Not for another month," Megan answered, rubbing her large belly. "But I was early with both of those two." She smiled at her sleeping kids.

"So, Lacey mentioned that you two aren't actually married. I hope I didn't cause you any discomfort."

"No." She sighed. She'd hoped that her little imaginary bubble wouldn't burst. Megan and Lacey knowing they weren't really married somehow deflated it a little. "Not at all."

"Todd and I were married when I was a few months along with Matthew," Megan answered.

"I hear a little Boston in your voice," she said finally.

She'd been dying to mention it earlier but had never gotten a moment alone with the woman.

"Yes." She chuckled. "I moved to Pride about a year before, when my brother Matthew died in a car accident."

Alice sobered. She couldn't imagine losing her brother Chris. They'd been so close, losing him would be like losing her best friend.

"I'm sorry," she said softly. Megan's eyes moved to her sleeping son.

"If it wasn't for that, I'd probably be dead," she said just as the truck doors opened and Todd and Eric climbed in.

"Telling her the story, eh?" Todd asked as he started the truck.

"I was about to." Megan smiled over at her husband.

"Story?" Eric asked.

"Of how we met." Todd chuckled. "Women love hearing love stories."

"Shush." Megan waved her husband off and started to tell her the story of how her brother, Matt, had died in a car crash, leaving her the big house and the B and B. Todd had been Matt's best friend and when she moved into the house, she fell in love with him.

"Of course, we were all set for our happy ever after when her ex showed up and kidnapped her," Todd added in. "She always leaves out that part."

Megan frowned and glanced at her sleeping kids. "That's because that darkness has no part in our bright lives."

"What happened?" Alice asked, leaning forward as she tried to imagine the very pregnant woman who was sitting in front of her being kidnapped while she was pregnant with the adorable boy sleeping next to her.

"Todd found me and rescued me," she added quickly.

"I found you, but you saved yourself," he corrected as he pulled into the parking area in front of the house. "She jumped out a hotel window to escape the bastard."

"Todd Jordan," Megan said quietly.

"They're asleep. They probably will be the rest of the night." Todd smiled and lifted his wife's hand to his lips. "Jordan women don't need rescuing. I knew then and there that we were meant to be."

"Oh?" Megan laughed. "It was that moment you realized it, was it?"

Alice could have sworn that he blushed, but he jumped out of the truck before she could check for sure.

CHAPTER 14

Eric finished hauling in the last load of groceries from the truck and set them on the countertop. Alice had put most of the things he'd already brought in away, but when he stepped inside this time and locked the door behind him, she had disappeared into the back.

Toeing off his boots, he hung his jacket and scarf and got busy putting the rest of the groceries away.

It was two days until Christmas and, still, the snow was continuing to fall outside. Some of it had melted during a brief sunny part of the day, but it had been too short-lived to melt much.

He threw a couple more logs on the fire, making sure to pull a few more in from the front porch, before going to look for her.

He found her soaking in a hot bathtub.

"Sorry." She smiled up at him. "I just couldn't get warm." She sighed and rested back. "Want to join me?"

He thought about it for a moment and decided the tub was far too small for him to squeeze into. He was pretty sure they would have to mop up most of the water from the floor if he even put a foot in with her.

"I don't think I'll fit." He sat next to the tub and leaned on the edge instead. He pulled off his shirt and tossed it onto the counter. "How about I wash your back?" And front and… his thoughts disappeared when she chuckled. The soft sexy sounds almost had him jumping into the water, regardless of the mess they'd make.

"Here." She handed him a cloth and poured soap into it as he held it. Then she leaned forward, exposing her back to his view.

He ran the cloth over her back, enjoying the soft sounds of pleasure she made as he went along. She'd pulled her dark hair up into a messy bun, so when she rested her head on her bent knees, he slowly washed her neck as well, taking his time to move the wisps of hair away so that they didn't get wet.

Then he cupped his hands and scooped up water to rinse her off, letting his fingertips trail over her skin until he noticed small goose bumps rising on her arms.

"Do you like that?" he asked, his voice cracking slightly.

"Very much." She glanced over her shoulder at him with a smile. "How about you do my front now?"

He sat back and watched her lie down, the water lapping over her breasts. His eyes were frozen on her.

"Well?" she said after a moment. "Here, let me get you started." She took his hand and laid it over one breast.

He swallowed hard and closed his eyes for just a second. "Alice," he said softly.

"Eric, touch me." Her hand covered his once more and forced it to start moving over her skin. He could feel her nipple through the washcloth and this time he was the one making the sounds of pure bliss.

She rolled her head back and rested it against the tub as his hands moved over her. His eyes moved to the apex of her legs. When he touched her and slid a finger into her, it took all of his willpower to stop himself from pulling her out of the water. Instead, he concentrated on pleasing her, watching her face as he built her up, mesmerized by the way her eyes turned, the way she bit her bottom lip and moved slowly under his hands. The water lapped at the edge of the bath as he bent over her, placing his lips gently over her lips as she cried out his name.

When she went completely lax, he gently picked her up out of the water. He wrapped her in a towel, carried her to the bedroom, and laid her on the bed. When he settled between her legs, using his mouth on her, she arched up and gripped his hair, crying out again.

"Eric," she gasped.

Chuckling, he lapped at her until she moaned his name. This time, he built her up but didn't let her fall alone. Instead, he climbed onto the bed after pulling off his jeans. As he filled her, he leaned close to her ear and whispered.

"I love you."

He felt her arms come around him, holding him to her as close as possible.

"I love you, too," she said, searching his eyes.

Smiling, he kissed her, showing her exactly how much he loved her.

After, they held onto each other once more. This time, he slipped into sleep, dreaming of the day they would have their own family.

When he woke, he could hear her moving around in

the kitchen area. She'd built a fire and was cooking French toast.

"Morning." He walked over and wrapped his arms around her.

"Morning." She smiled up at him. "I thought I'd cook this morning." She handed him a cup of coffee. "The weather report says we're supposed to get a break in the snow today." She motioned towards the muted television.

He walked over with his coffee and turned on the sound. Sure enough, the new report stated that they would have a break in the weather for the next two days.

He stood there with his coffee mug forgotten in his hands as he thought about them heading in two separate directions in life. What would happen? He'd drop Alice off at her parents' place and go over to his sister's. They'd be apart for Christmas. He'd never get the chance to make those plans with her he'd been hoping to.

"Is everything okay?" she asked. He heard the eagerness in her voice and avoided her eyes.

"Sure." He turned off the television. "I guess this means we can head to Portland now." He walked over and sat down at the table.

"If we want," she answered. "The main roads probably won't be clear for a few hours after the sun comes out. Who knows about the smaller roads off of highway one-oh-one." She set a plate of French toast in front of him.

He hadn't thought of that. "We can go for a short drive for lunch if you want, to test things out?"

"Sure." She was still acting relaxed, as if leaving the cabin, going in separate directions, wouldn't faze her at all, so he kept the conversation light during breakfast. They kept the television off and talked about all of the snow outside.

She told him a story about the last time she'd seen snow, and they talked about going sledding with Chris when they were kids.

He couldn't remember a winter they hadn't pulled out their plastic sleds and climbed the hill behind their neighborhood with the rest of the kids on their street.

"Remember when Chris broke his wrist before winter break?" he asked, laughing.

"He was so upset Mom wouldn't let him go sledding, so he snuck out and we all went." She laughed.

"He duct-taped a pillow around his cast just in case." He chuckled remembering how big Chris's arm was in that thing. "But it worked. He flew off the sled and landed without even hurting it."

During a short walk to the beach, they talked about school and family.

When they were walking back up the cleared path towards their cabin, Alice turned to him.

"Do you think Chris and Dawn will get married?" she asked.

He shrugged. "I'm not sure. I mean, the last time I went out with them, they were pretty serious."

She sighed and stopped at the foot of the stairs. "What do you think of Dawn? I mean, I've met her once, but…" She bit her bottom lip.

"Hey." He took her shoulders and looked into her eyes. "She's great. Really. None of my warning bells go off with her."

"Oh, well…" She smiled. "We all know just how great your warning bells are" She tilted her head and he knew what was coming. “I think her name was Krista?” He groaned.

“Shut up,” he said, chuckling. He pulled her closer and tried to kiss her, but she dodged him.

“Then there was Eva and Tiffany and—”

He shut her up by covering her laughter with his mouth.

“It’s the one I have now that matters the most,” he said to her. “You’re what I’ve been working my way up to.”

CHAPTER 15

Alice could tell that Eric was deep in thought as they pulled the car out of the bed and breakfast's parking area. Todd had been out there earlier and had cleared away most of the snow. Even the drive out to the main road had been cleared already.

"So," he asked, looking at the road in front of them. "Which direction?"

"Well, I'd like another look at the town." She thought about it. "Since it's Christmas Eve, maybe we can walk through the lights again. I didn't snap any pictures the other day."

"Sure." He nodded and turned in the direction of town instead of the main highway.

They drove around the small town, enjoying the homes and the coastline views. He took a road that led them to a little dock area where fishing boats bobbed up and down in the cold water.

They drove past the town, but a few miles outside, the road was blocked off still by highway signs.

"Guess that answers that," Eric said, maneuvering the car until they were heading back towards Pride.

"It would probably be safer to wait, anyway," she added, thankful that they would be spending Christmas in Pride.

"Will it be so bad? Spending Christmas here?" he asked as they came around the corner and the small town came into sight again.

The sun was shining down on the town as if a sunbeam had been made especially for that moment.

"No," she answered with a smile. "I couldn't imagine a better place to spend Christmas."

He reached over and took her hand in his. "Or someone better to spend it with," he added.

When they hit the outskirts of town again, she noticed that all of the lights were on in the town square. Finding a parking spot in front of the drug store, he parked and looked up and down the quiet streets.

"Let's walk a little," he said, turning off the car. "I can't believe how magical this place looks," he said before getting out of the car.

"As I said before, I don't want to leave," she said as she got out. She was relieved that the road was closed.

Hand in hand, they started walking through the town square again. This time, they were the only ones around. The trees were weighted down with the heavy snow, but still the lights dangled and glowed from the branches.

She knew it had eaten at him this morning after they found out there was a break in the weather, thinking that they would be heading to their own families for Christmas.

No matter what happened, she would have made sure

they had spent time together. Even if it meant ditching her family.

As they walked down the pathway, her mind wandered to what could have been. She shivered, not because of the cold, but because of the possibility of having been stuck in a hotel along I-5 instead of here. When Eric felt her shiver, he pulled her closer and wrapped his arms around her.

"Cold?" he asked.

"No." She sighed. "Just thankful I turned off highway five."

He chuckled. "I am as well. Very."

They stopped in the middle of the square and looked around. The town was even more beautiful now that the sky was clear and blue. There were still a few puffy clouds drifting by but, for the most part, it was a perfect day.

It reminded her of a perfect little snow-globe world, one blanketed in crisp clean snow.

The pathways had been cleared earlier and since the snow had stopped and the sun had made a slight appearance, warming the pavement, they were clear of all snow and ice.

"Can you imagine living in a place like this? I bet they have Fourth of July parades and homecoming dances here," she said, looking around the town.

"Family barbeques," he added. "Town meetings." He laughed, half-joking. "I mean, it's straight out of the movies."

"Yeah, all the old ones our mothers love watching." She turned to him, remembering all of the times she'd watched the black-and-white movies with her mother and his. "We should bring them here. This summer. We can rent out all of the cabins and…" She turned away when her face flushed. She'd been thinking about how perfect the town was to get married in.

She could see it clearly: Putting up their families in the cabins. Setting up the town square for a wedding. Or better yet, having a beach wedding in the warm sand.

"What?" he asked, turning her back towards him.

"Nothing." She shook her head.

"Alice." He used a gloved finger to pull her chin up until their eyes met. She could see that he wasn't going to drop it. She knew him too well and knew that there wasn't any way of avoiding telling him her thoughts.

"It's just… I was thinking that I bet it would make a great place for a wedding."

He stilled and then smiled. "You want to get married here?" he asked, looking around.

"Here"—she avoided his gaze again—"or on the beach by the cabins." She shrugged, trying to sound casual.

"Okay," he said, surprising her.

"Okay?" she asked, unsure what he was saying.

"Sure." He shrugged. "I mean, where else would we get married but the place we fell in love?" He pulled her closer to him. "So?" He waited. "What do you think?"

"I…" She blinked a few times, her heart racing so fast she could almost hear it in her ears. "Are you asking me to marry you?" she finally asked.

He smiled at her. "I would get down on my knee, but…" He glanced at the still-wet sidewalk. "Maybe later."

She didn't need him on his knees. All she'd ever wanted was a moment this perfect. Looking around now, she realized it was more than that. It was pure magic.

"Yes," she answered easily. "Of course, I'll marry you. I've been waiting my entire life for you to ask me. Yes," she said again before throwing herself into his arms and kissing him.

Seven months later

Alice held her breath as she started down the sandy pathway. She nervously played with the flowers in her hands as she walked closer and closer to the small crowd.

Surrounded by her family, she stopped in front of Eric and her brother, who was acting as his best man.

Eric's sister, Sarah, was standing in as her maid of honor. She had a few friends she'd thought of for the job, but none of them had known her as long as Sarah had. Besides, they had grown a lot closer in the past few months since she'd moved back to Portland.

"Hi," Eric said under his breath.

"Hi," she replied and smiled at him.

"Want to get married?" he asked with a chuckle.

"Yes." She laughed, as did the small group of people surrounding them.

The ceremony was short, since they hadn't wanted any of the bells and whistles. Besides, they had officially gotten married at the courthouse in Portland the day they'd gotten home, a week after Christmas.

She'd transferred her credits up to the University of Portland and had gotten another internship at the Veterans Affairs clinic in town. She'd already been offered a job. Several, actually.

Eric had taken a position with his father's old employer as head engineer, since his father's buddy had retired.

They were in the process of house hunting but had

wanted to take a weekend to celebrate their marriage with their families.

The Jordans had helped plan their special day and several of them were in attendance, including Todd and Megan's newest daughter, Susannah, or Suzie, as they called the tiny baby.

Suzie and her older sister Sara were dressed in matching dresses. They sat by their very uncomfortable older brother, Matthew, who was dressed in a little suit.

Alice had thought about making Sara one of her flower girls, but she was still a little too young. Instead, Eric's nephews had played ushers and, with the help of their fathers, they sat everyone in the folding chairs.

Most of the guests were dressed casual enough to enjoy a warm day on the beach. Even her dress was short enough, hitting just below her knees. She'd kicked off her sandals as she'd stepped off the pathway and had enjoyed the warm sand between her toes as she'd made her way towards the wedding party.

She glanced around and smiled at the Jordan family in attendance. She'd never been anywhere before where she'd felt so welcomed, so accepted. Even her family had fallen for the small town.

Their rehearsal dinner last night had been at the main house at the bed and breakfast, with Iian, Todd's brother, as head chef. She'd enjoyed the relaxed atmosphere and had loved returning to the cabin where she and Eric had spent those two weeks trapped together in the snow.

Since there were going to be a lot more people at the wedding reception, it was taking place at the Golden Oar, the Jordan's family-owned restaurant in town. The place had a reputation as one of the best restaurants to eat in along the Oregon coast. She'd never had better food than with Todd's brother Iian cooking.

Eric squeezed her hand again as they said their vows once more. They had practiced them so many times in the past few weeks that she knew them by heart. They had decided to write their own words, which had made her nervous at first, but then she'd decided to keep it simple and just tell him exactly how she felt.

"I've loved you for as long as I can remember," she started out. "I've dreamed of the day when I would become your wife. The day when we'd be together forever. The day I would become yours and you would become mine. I love you," she said as he smiled at her.

"Alice, you blindsided me." The crowd chuckled as he smiled at her. "I didn't think it was possible to love someone so much. I think about you day and night. I want to be with you every waking moment, holding you. I've never been as happy as I am now, but I plan on having a lifetime full of these moments, with you," he added. "I'm so glad we were snowed in together." The crowd chuckled again. "It was the perfect storm."

When Eric kissed her, their family cheered, and she knew her life was going to be exactly what she'd dreamed it would be.

This is a work of fiction. Names, characters, places, and incidents either are the product of the author's imagination or are used fictitiously, and any resemblance to actual persons, living or dead, business establishments, events or locales is entirely coincidental.

A PRIDE CHRISTMAS

DIGITAL ISBN: 978-1-945100-05-5

PRINT ISBN:

Copyright © 2019 Jill Sanders

All rights reserved.

Copyeditor: Erica Ellis – inkdeepediting.com

No part of this book may be reproduced, scanned, or distributed in any printed or electronic form without permission. Please do not participate in or encourage piracy of copyrighted materials in violation of the author's rights. Purchase only authorized editions.

ALSO BY JILL SANDERS

The Pride Series

Finding Pride

Discovering Pride

Returning Pride

Lasting Pride

Serving Pride

Red Hot Christmas

My Sweet Valentine

Return To Me

Rescue Me

The Secret Series

Secret Seduction

Secret Pleasure

Secret Guardian

Secret Passions

Secret Identity

Secret Sauce

The West Series

Loving Lauren

Taming Alex

Holding Haley

Missy's Moment

Breaking Travis

Roping Ryan

Wild Bride

Corey's Catch

Tessa's Turn

The Grayton Series

Last Resort

Someday Beach

Rip Current

In Too Deep

Swept Away

High Tide

Lucky Series

Unlucky In Love

Sweet Resolve

Best of Luck

A Little Luck

Silver Cove Series

Silver Lining

French Kiss

Happy Accident

Hidden Charm

A Silver Cove Christmas

Entangled Series – Paranormal Romance

The Awakening

The Beckoning

The Ascension

Haven, Montana Series

Closer to You

Never Let Go

Holding On

Pride Oregon Series

A Dash of Love

My Kind of Love

Season of Love

Tis the Season

Dare to Love

Where I Belong

Wildflowers Series

Summer Nights

Summer Heat

Stand Alone Books

Twisted Rock

For a complete list of books:

http://JillSanders.com

ABOUT THE AUTHOR

Jill Sanders is a New York Times, USA Today, and international bestselling author of Sweet Contemporary Romance, Romantic Suspense, Western Romance, and Paranormal Romance novels. With over 55 books in eleven series, translations into several different languages, and audiobooks there's plenty to choose from. Look for Jill's bestselling stories wherever romance books are sold or visit her at jillsanders.com

Jill comes from a large family with six siblings, including an identical twin. She was raised in the Pacific Northwest and later relocated to Colorado for college and a successful IT career before discovering her talent for writing sweet and sexy page-turners. After Colorado, she decided to move south, living in Texas and now making her home along the Emerald Coast of Florida. You will find that the settings of several of her series are inspired by her time spent living in these areas. She has two sons and offset the testosterone in her house by adopting three furry little ladies that provide her company while she's locked in her writing cave. She enjoys heading to the beach, hiking, swimming, wine-tasting, and pickleball with her husband, and of course writing. If you have read any of her books, you may also notice that there is a love of food, especially sweets! She has been blamed for a few added pounds by her assistant, editor, and fans... donuts or pie anyone?

facebook.com/JillSandersBooks

twitter.com/JillMSanders

bookbub.com/authors/jill-sanders

Made in the USA
Coppell, TX
15 April 2021

53760532R00073